When Bolt returned to Penny's room at the Barbary Hotel, he knocked lightly on the door, called out his name so he wouldn't frighten her, then opened the door and stepped inside.

"I got it," he announced, holding the sack of food up for her to see. He looked over at the bed. His heart skipped a beat when he saw that it was empty. He looked around the small room as if he expected her to be there. Then he studied the room carefully, saw no sign of a struggle. Her clothes were gone and so was she. It was that simple.

He waited for more than an hour before he headed back to the Pelican Point Hotel. If Penny had been kidnapped again, he wouldn't know where to begin looking for her. And he had no clues to her disappearance except the name "Jubal."

His thoughts shifted to Valerie Blair. She was in danger, too, he knew, but again, his only clue was the man with the limp. It wasn't much to go on in this big city. . . .

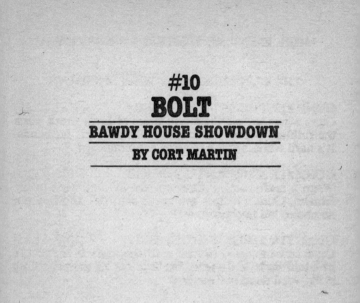

#10
BOLT
BAWDY HOUSE SHOWDOWN
BY CORT MARTIN

ZEBRA BOOKS
KENSINGTON PUBLISHING CORP.

ZEBRA BOOKS

are published by

KENSINGTON PUBLISHING CORP.
475 Park Avenue South
New York, N.Y. 10016

Copyright © 1983 by Cort Martin

Printed in the United States of America

Chapter One

Jared Bolt stood at the open window of his room at the Pelican Point Hotel and let the cool sea breeze wash against his face. He looked down from the second-floor window, awed by the vast expanse of the Pacific Ocean below, mesmerized by the constant rumbling of the ocean waves pounding against the shoreline of the Barbary Coast. He took a deep breath, smelled the mystery and intrigue that seemed to float ashore on the ocean breezes.

There was something about the town of San Francisco that excited him. Something that made his blood race, his heart pound faster.

His eyes focused on a small boat that bobbed up and down on the water as it headed for the shore around the bend, just out of Bolt's view. He strained his eyes, tried to see who was in the boat. Just before it disappeared from sight, he counted eight or nine people aboard. At least two of them were men, but the others appeared to be women. It was hard to tell from that distance. He wondered who they were, where they had come from, where they were going. Not that it mattered. He didn't know a soul in San Francisco except his long-time friend, Tom Penrod, who had ridden in with him to the Barbary Coast early that afternoon, not more than an hour ago.

After spending some time in Texas during the winter, Bolt and Tom had headed west to the golden state, California, a place where neither of them had been before. They had picked up the old Butterfield Overland Mail route in Tucson, followed it to Fort Yuma and then to Los Angeles. Sticking to the old Butterfield trail after leaving the city of the angels, it had taken them five days of riding through rough, beautiful mountain country to reach the bay area. Just south of San Francisco, they cut west again and followed the coastline until they found themselves on a high cliff overlooking the ocean. From there they spotted the Pelican Point Hotel, a rambling resort that sprawled out across the rolling land next to the ocean.

As Bolt gazed at the hypnotic expanse of the ocean, he saw a large sailing ship out on the horizon. A schooner or windjammer. Ships held a special fascination for him. He had always wanted to sail across the ocean to another country. A boyhood dream of lazy summers. That was one of the reasons he had been drawn to the Barbary Coast.

A smaller boat, much like the one he'd seen minutes before, was near the big sailing ship, heading toward the shore. The smaller boat was a long way out, but it appeared to be loaded down with passengers. It looked like passengers of the larger

6

ship were being transferred to the smaller boat out in the ocean and then transported to shore. Maybe the boat he'd seen earlier had collected its passengers from the ship, too, but it didn't make sense. Why wouldn't the big sailing vessel come in closer to the shore and drop anchor if it wanted to discharge passengers? Maybe the wind was too much to maneuver the rig along the shoreline. Or maybe there was a coral reef or dangerous rock formation underneath the water that Bolt couldn't see.

His curiosity aroused, Bolt's mind was filled with thoughts when he heard the knock on the door. He turned his head, looked across the room at the closed door, heard his friend's voice.

"Bolt? You ready to go?" called Tom Penrod from the hallway.

"Yeah, come on in."

Tom opened the door and stepped inside the room. Although he had cleaned up, washed the trail dust off him and changed shirts, his hair didn't look like it had been combed in a week. But then, it never looked like he combed it. He refused to use hair tonic or grease on it, and without it the strands of hair wouldn't stay in place.

"We made it, Tom," Bolt said, turning back to the open window.

"Yair. Two country bumpkins make good in the big city. I can see the headlines now."

"You joke, but we're going to open the classiest bawdy house this side of the Mississippi! The people of San Francisco are supposed to be wealthy, full of culture. High society and all that. But you and I are

7

going to show them what real class is all about."

"Yeah, sure, but if we don't get something to eat soon, we won't make it to opening night."

"How can you think about eating at a time like this? This is what we've been waiting for. Our golden opportunity!"

"After eating your cooking for the last three weeks, it ain't hard to think about food!"

"Just look at that ocean out there, would you? Smell the salt water! Did you ever see so much water in your life?"

Tom stepped over to the window and stood beside his friend. He was a couple of inches shorter than Bolt, but the difference in height wasn't noticeable unless they were standing next to each other. They both had about the same build, but Bolt's frame was solid, with whipcord muscles. Tom was equally as strong, but he was slightly slimmer, with a wiry body. Bolt's dark hair didn't have the natural curl that Tom's had and he usually wore it fairly long and shaggy.

"Hell, a man could starve to death while you stand there gawking at an oversized mud puddle," Tom grumbled.

"Where's your sense of adventure? Look at that ship way out there on the horizon. Wouldn't you love to be aboard it right now, sailing around the world?"

"Hell, if the chow was good, I wouldn't give a damn where I was going."

"Tom, look at that smaller boat, heading toward shore. See it off to the left?"

Tom stepped closer, saw the boat that bobbed in the ocean waters. "Yeah, I see it."

8

"Looks like there are two men rowing the boat and about six women passengers, doesn't it? Damn, I wish I had my binoculars."

"I'll be damned, you learned to count! You're right. Six gals and two lucky fellers. Now that's my kind of odds. Three to one."

"I'm curious, Tom. That's the second boat full of women I've seen heading toward shore in the last ten minutes. What do you suppose they're doing out there?"

"Obviously, they're going for a boat ride. People do that out here, I'm told." Tom's tone was sarcastic.

"Could be, but I think they might be coming off that big sailing ship out there."

"So what does that prove?"

"Not a damn thing. Just curious. Watch that boat. See, it's heading for shore, but it's disappearing around that bend. Damn! I wish I knew what was around there." Bolt watched the small boat until it was out of sight.

"Bolt, I think you're just looking for trouble."

"I don't have to look for it," he laughed. "It usually finds me."

"Well, I'm going to rustle up some grub," Tom said. "You goin' with me or not?"

"I'm coming," Bolt said. "Do you want to eat here at the hotel or ride on in to town?"

"We came to see the big city, didn't we?"

"Damn right. Let's go."

Bolt and Tom went downstairs, out the back door of the hotel, walked along the flower-lined path to the stables out back that were provided for the guests. They saddled up their horses, got directions to a good restaurant from the stable boy and headed in for their first look at the town of San Francisco.

The Hilltop House was an elegant restaurant located at the top of one of the many hilly streets in the middle of town. It was right next door to the San Francisco Opera House and drew the opera crowds who dined there before the opera or came there after the performances for drinks or late-evening suppers.

The restaurant was not crowded this time of day. It was still too early for the opera patrons to dine before going to the theatre. The waiter, who was dressed in a black tuxedo and stiff white shirt, seated Bolt and Tom at a window table and gave them a menu that was hand-printed in ornate script.

"Fancy place," said Bolt, glancing at the elegant decor.

"With fancy prices," said Tom, glancing at the menu.

"Yeah, and not a bad view."

Tom glanced out the window and saw what Bolt meant. Three extremely beautiful girls walked along the boardwalk just outside the window.

"Looking better all the time," Tom grinned.

"They look like show girls to me," said Bolt.

"So maybe I'll get some culture while we're here. I wouldn't mind going to the opera if that's the kind of stuff they're offering."

"This might not be a bad place to settle down for a couple of years. We'll find a place to open our bordello and then maybe we can find us a modest ocean front home. Hire someone else to run the business and buy us a little boat."

"Yeah, you talk like that and you might even find

yourself taking a wife."

"No, I draw the line there. I'm not ready to settle down yet."

They ate an elegant meal of steak and fresh seafood, washed it down with expensive wine. They watched the people stroll by, talked of their plans. When they were almost through eating, Bolt noticed a girl walking on the other side of the street.

"Now there's my type," he said. "Tall, willowy, dark hair. I'll bet she even has blue eyes."

He watched the girl as she turned into one of the stores. A yardage store that boasted of imported fabrics, according to the signs in the windows. As Bolt sipped his wine, idly watching the front of the yardage store for another glimpse at the pretty lady, he saw a tall lanky man with a slight limp walk along the boardwalk, turn into the yardage store.

"Doesn't seem the type to be buying fancy fabrics, does he?" Bolt said.

"What in the hell are you talking about?" Tom said, spreading butter on a biscuit before taking a bite.

"The fellow that just went in the yardage store. Didn't you see him?"

"Nope. There's times when food is more important than watching strange pussy."

"He looked like a bum in those tight brown pants, and that black baggy jacket. He had his hat brim pulled down low as if he was hiding his face."

"No law against that, is there? He's probably in there buying some material for his bitch wife."

"He looked like a hardcase to me."

"No law against that either. I swear, you're gonna

think yourself right into trouble again.''

As Bolt sipped his wine, watching for the girl to come out of the store, he saw something that startled him. A cloud of dark smoke billowed up inside one of the windows of the yardage store.

''Tom, you see that smoke over there?''

''Where?''

''Across the street! Where the girl is! That damned building's on fire!''

Tom looked across the street.

''It sure is!''

Just as he said it, both windows in the front of the building exploded from the heat that had built up inside. There was a loud explosion, the shattering of glass as they blew out, crashing to the street. A ball of fire rolled across the floor inside the building, shot up in the air.

Bolt jumped up, ran for the door.

''The girl's still in there!''

Other customers in the restaurant got up, followed Bolt and Tom outside to see what was happening.

As Bolt dashed across the street, he saw a short, stocky man running out of the store, his clothes ablaze. The man screamed in pain as the heat seared his flesh.

People ran out of nearby buildings. A crowd was already forming in the street, on the boardwalk by the time Bolt got to the other side of the street.

''Tom, take care of that man. I'm going in after the girl!''

''Give me your jacket!'' Tom ordered one of the bystanders.

The burning man waved his arms in the air in

desperation, but that only fanned the flames on his shirt sleeves.

"Is the girl still in there?" Bolt yelled to the man.

"Yes ... but you ... can't go in ... there. I couldn't ... get her out. God! Help me! Please someone help me!"

"What about the man?" Bolt asked. "The other customer?"

"Ran out ... back ..." gasped the burning man, "the ... coward!"

Tom pushed him to the ground, rolled him over, grabbed the jacket from the onlooker and wrapped it around the man to smother the flames.

Bolt started inside the building. The heat was intense and the smoke was so thick he couldn't see anything inside. He pulled his jacket collar up, covered his nose and mouth to keep from breathing the smoke. He crouched low, made his way through the smoke-filled room. The flames were on one side of the room, eating at one wall, consuming bolts of fabric.

"Miss! Miss, where are you?" he called. Squinting his eyes, he scanned as much of the floor area that he could see through the smoke, looking for the girl. He couldn't see her anywhere.

The smoke filtered through to his nostrils. He tried to hold his breath and when he finally took a breath, he started coughing and choking. The smoke burned his throat.

He dropped clear down to the floor, crawled on his hands and knees toward the back of the room, keeping his head as low as he could.

"Lady! Where are you?" he called again.

He heard a faint cry. Then a cough.

She was still alive! If he could only get to her and get her out of there before the whole building went up in flames.

The smoke billowed up before him and for a brief instant, he could see a few feet in front of him. He got a glimpse of her feet, her dress. She was sprawled out on the floor in front of one of the counters. He scooted across the floor toward her.

When he was six feet away, a flaming bolt of fabric fell off the counter, landed right in front of him, blocking his way to the girl. The flame leaped out, touched the bottom of her full blue skirt.

The girl coughed again, tried to stand up, tried to retreat from the flames that licked at the front of her dress.

"Stay low!" Bolt called. "I'll get you out!"

As the flames lapped at the hem of her skirt, the girl choked and gagged, crumpled to the floor. She was unconscious, barely breathing.

Bolt jumped up, ran around the bolt of cloth, ripping off his jacket as he ran. When he got to her, he slapped the jacket over the bottom of her dress, held it tight to smother the flames. She didn't move at all. She no longer coughed or made a sound. He couldn't tell if she was still alive.

He wrapped the jacket around her head, picked her up quickly and threw her over his shoulder like a sack of potatoes. He turned, started for the front door. Flames had spread across the front of the room, making it almost impossible to reach the door. He looked toward the back, but the smoke was so thick, he couldn't even see the back entrance. Just as he was about to move toward the back of the building, a flaming beam fell across his path. He was totally blocked by flames on three sides and flames began to attack both ends of the remaining wall.

He coughed and sputtered, knew he had to get out of there fast. He knew he had only one choice. He had to make a run for the front door. He had to risk going through the rows of burning bolts of fabric. He had to risk running through the smoke that could choke both of them to death. Even if he made it past the flaming material, the burning shelves and wall, there was no guarantee that he could get out alive. The walls could go at any minute. The whole burning building could collapse on him in an instant.

The smoke stung his eyes as he looked toward the front of the building. As the smoke billowed around him, he couldn't even tell where the front door was anymore. He became confused. Then as the smoke curled around and changed direction, he finally saw the flaming outline of the front door.

He held his breath, made a dash for the opening. Sheer guts drove him through the flames that reached out for his pantlegs. The flames leaped up shoulder high all around him and he felt the heat penetrate his flesh. He kept on running, not giving the flames a chance to set his clothing on fire.

He was in the thick of the smoke, about ten feet from the front door, when the whole front wall of the building collapsed in front of him. Burning boards folded on top of each other, forming a wall of flames fifteen feet high.

He stopped short, all exits blocked. He and the girl were trapped inside a burning coffin.

Chapter Two

Bolt had to find a way out of the burning building right away. If he hesitated for even a brief moment, both he and the girl he carried over his shoulder would be consumed by the deadly fire. Already, he found it difficult to breathe. If he was overcome by the smoke, neither one of them would get out alive.

A blast of heat rushed toward him when the front of the building collapsed. He felt the heat penetrate through his clothing, causing his skin to tingle. His throat was parched and it felt like his lungs were on fire.

He dashed to his left, headed for the front corner of the building where the flames were not so high. Holding the girl tightly, he leaped over the burning boards at the corner. The flames reached up for his legs, but he managed to escape through the only opening without getting burned. He carried the girl to the boardwalk, a safe distance from the burning building. Tom Penrod rushed up, helped him set the girl down gently on the ground.

"Is she alive?" Tom asked.

"I don't know," Bolt said, still coughing. He jerked the jacket from her head, looked down at her face. Her eyes were closed, her body limp. He leaned down closer, checked to see if he could detect signs of her breathing. He slipped his hand under her head, lifted it slightly. He patted her cheeks, begged her to speak to him.

Her eyes fluttered open. She coughed, nearly strangled on the smoke that was trapped in her lungs.

"Thank God!" Bolt said, wiping his brow.

The crowd of onlookers tried to press in closer to see the girl. They started talking to each other in excited voices.

"Move back," Tom ordered. "Give her air."

"Wha ... what happened?" the girl muttered between coughs. Her blue eyes blinked from the effects of the smoke as she looked up at Bolt. "Who ... who are you?"

"The name's Bolt. Jared Bolt. You had a close call, ma'am. You all right?"

She tried to sit up, saw the scorched hem of her dress, the gaping hole at the bottom of the dress where the fire burned through the material.

"The fire!" she said as she remembered. She looked up at Bolt. "You saved my life, didn't you?"

"I reckon so."

"Thank you, Mr. Bolt," she said in a soft voice. "I owe you a great deal."

"I was just at the right place at the right time," he smiled. "Anyone would have done the same." But Bolt knew that wasn't true. He had seen the crowd of people who had gathered in the street when the fire

17

started. Not one of them had made any attempt to rescue her from the flaming building. They had just stood there watching the building burn, basking in the excitement. No one had lifted a finger to help him or Tom. But he didn't hold that against them. People reacted differently to a crisis.

"What about Mister Talbott?" the girl asked, glancing over at the flaming boards at the front of the building. "Is he . . . is he still in there?"

"Who's Talbott?" Bolt said.

"The store owner. I was near the back of the store when I noticed that the place was on fire. I knew Mr. Talbott was up front, but the smoke was so thick I couldn't see him. Is he . . .?"

"Mr. Talbott's all right, Miss," Tom said. "One of his arms got burned pretty bad but he'll make it. We took him over to Doc Swenson's office."

"Thank God he's still alive. He's the nicest old man." It was hard for the girl to talk without coughing.

"Do you want to go to the doctor, Miss. . . ?" Bolt said.

"Blair. Valerie Blair. No thanks. My throat hurts and my eyes burn like crazy, but I think I'm all right, thanks to you. I just want to go home."

"If you're sure . . ."

"Yes. Would you mind taking me home, Mr. Bolt. I'd like to thank you properly for saving my life." She smiled up at him.

"If you'll drop the Mister, I'd be pleased to take you home," Bolt said, returning her warm smile.

He wondered where she lived, whether she was married. But more than anything, he wondered if

18

there was a special meaning to her smile. Bolt looked into Valerie Blair's eyes. They were the bluest blue he'd ever seen. Her cheeks were drained of color from the shock of being in the burning building. Her long dark brown hair that fell around her face and shoulders only made her cheeks look paler. Her body trembled now that she was outside, safe from the searing flames.

"I'd be grateful," she said.

"You sure you're all right?"

"Just a little shaky," she said, her voice a low husk. She folded her arms across her chest, rubbed her arms with her hands to warm herself. "I didn't realize how scared I was until now."

Bolt wrapped his jacket around her shoulders, helped her to her feet.

"Will you be able to ride double with me?" he asked.

"I have my own horse and buggy which I'll have to take home. Could you take me in that? It's on the corner, in front of Johnson's Meat and Fish Market. I came to town to pick up an order of meat. I just stopped in at the yardage store to get some lace for a dress I'm making, but I guess I won't get the lace now. Poor Mr. Talbott. He's lost everything." She looked up at the burning building, shook her head sadly.

"Not his life."

The onlookers had finally formed a bucket brigade to put out the fire, keep it from spreading to other buildings, using water from a community watering trough. Already the flames were beginning to die out as they doused the fire with the water.

"Tom, go get our horses and take them down to Miss Blair's buggy on the corner. We'll meet you there."

"What about our supper? We didn't pay for it."

"I'll take care of it later, after I get Miss Blair home."

As Bolt walked Valerie to her buggy, she felt faint, grabbed his arm for support. He wrapped his arm around her waist, held her close to him. He felt her lithe body lean into him. She was about five inches shorter than he was, with a trim graceful figure that felt good beside him.

When they reached her spotless buggy and well-groomed horse, Bolt helped her up on the seat. Her body was light and supple when he lifted her up. His hand brushed against a soft breast but she didn't seem to notice.

"I'm sorry about your dress, Miss Blair," he said when he saw the black scorched area at the bottom of the front of her dress where part of it had burned away.

"Please call me Valerie. All my friends do. And don't worry about my dress. I can fix that. I'm just grateful to be alive."

"Do you want me to run in and pick up your order of meat?"

"If you wouldn't mind. It will be charged to my account so I don't have to pay for it now. I'm putting you to so much trouble already. I don't even like to ask you to take me home, but I feel so dizzy."

"No trouble, Valerie. I'll get the meat."

"I'll make it up to you somehow," she said, her smile melting Bolt's heart. She had dimples when she smiled and it was all Bolt could do to take his eyes off her.

When Bolt came out of the meat market with the box of meat packages, he noticed the man standing beside the buggy, talking to Valerie. It was the same man he'd seen enter the yardage store after Valerie went in. The same tight brown pants, the baggy black jacket. The battered hat was pushed back on his head now. As Bolt approached the buggy, the man tipped his hat to the girl, pulled it back down low on his forehead and limped away.

Tom pulled up behind the buggy, riding his own horse, leading Bolt's by the reins. Bolt told him to follow the buggy with both horses, then he climbed up in the seat beside Valerie.

"Valerie, who was that man who was talking to you just now?"

"I don't know. He just walked up and said he was concerned about me and offered to take me home."

"Did you know he was inside the yardage store when the fire started?" Valerie looked at Bolt with puzzled blue eyes.

"No. I knew someone had come in the store. I heard Mr. Talbott say 'Good afternoon' to someone, but I was at the back of the store looking at the different rolls of lace on the shelf. I didn't turn around."

"What happened in there? How did the fire get started?" Bolt didn't have anything to base his feelings on, but he had the odd feeling that somehow the man with the limp was involved in the fire. Probably just coincidence, but why would the man show up again? Unless he was concerned about

21

Valerie, as she had said.

"I really don't know. I heard a crash, then when I looked around, all I could see was the smoke in the front of the store. Right after that, a big ball of fire seemed to roll across the floor. The smoke became so thick, I couldn't see a thing. I started to feel my way along the counter, trying to make it to the front door, but the smoke got worse. The flames were coming toward me. I guess I passed out. The last thing I remember was hearing Mr. Talbott screaming. Oh, I can't think about it anymore. But, I don't think that man had anything to do with setting the building on fire. I think he was just trying to help."

Bolt noticed that she was wringing her hands in her lap, that her cheeks were paler than before. She looked like a delicate china doll.

"You're probably right. Now, where do you live?"

"Turn right at the first street and then take that next road up the hill. It winds around, runs into another road up a piece. Follow that road. We live on the top of the hill."

"This town has more hills than I've ever seen," Bolt said. But he was thinking about something else. She had said "we." Now he knew she didn't live alone.

From the seat, Bolt snapped the reins, urged Valerie's horse out into the street. He followed her directions which led them up a road that curved up to a section of San Francisco where there were several plush estates with elegant homes and neatly manicured lawns, lush green trees and flowers in bloom. Valerie snuggled in close to him, said very little until they reached the top of the hill.

Bolt's mind was filled with thoughts of the hauntingly beautiful girl beside him. He wondered who she lived with, wondered if she was married. He tried to remember how she had introduced herself. She hadn't said "Miss Blair," she had said "Valerie Blair." As he looked around at the expensive homes on the hill, he knew she was wealthy. He should have known. She had that special quality that came, not from wealth, but from a gracious upbringing.

"That's my home over there," she said as she sat up straight, moved away from Bolt, pointed to her right.

"Nice home."

"You're new in town, aren't you?" Valerie said, giving Bolt a sideways glance as she straightened her skirt around her.

"Does it show?" he smiled.

"Yes," she giggled. "Besides, I would have remembered you if I'd seen you before. Where are you from?"

"Everyplace and noplace."

Valerie tilted her head, gave him a quizzical look.

"A drifter, hmmm?" she teased.

"I've been called worse."

"Where are you staying?"

"At the Pelican Point Hotel."

"Well, at least you've got good taste. That's the most exclusive hotel in town."

"Didn't know that. We just stumbled across it on our way into San Francisco."

"Romantic out there. I mean, with the view of the ocean. There's something magical about the water, the sea breeze." She smiled, a dreamy look in her eyes.

23

Desire flooded Bolt's loins when she smiled. He knew she was flirting with him by the twinkle in her eyes, the way she tilted her head when she looked at him.

"That's why we're staying out there."

"Because it's romantic?"

"No. Because I like the ocean, the water, the coast-line."

"Appears we like the same things. I've been there for a couple of social events, but I'd like to spend more time out there, just to enjoy the view."

Bolt looked away, cleared the husk from his voice. He pulled the horse and buggy into the circular drive-way, stopped right in front of the house. He felt her eyes still on him.

"You married, Valerie?" he asked bluntly.

"No. Do I look it?" she giggled.

"I wouldn't know about that."

"I'm only eighteen. I live here with my parents. My father won't allow me to marry until I'm at least twenty-one. He's very strict with me. And very particular about the men who come to court me."

Bolt recognized the challenge in her eyes, the hunger. He'd seen the look before. It seemed that the more protective the father was, the more eager the daughter was to explore her own blossoming sexuality.

"And you go along with whatever your father says."

"Yes. Not that I always agree with him, but he's a very respected man in this community and I wouldn't do anything to hurt him or his reputation. There are times, though, when I wish I weren't the daughter of

24

Rodney F. Blair. Not that I don't love my father, my parents. It's just they treat me like a little girl and I'm all grown up now. With grown-up feelings and . . . and grown-up . . . needs. You married, Bolt?" She took a deep breath and when she looked at Bolt again, her blue eyes held the same magnetic fascination for him that the ocean waters had before.

"Nope. What does your father do?" he asked.

"He's the president of the San Francisco Mercantile Bank. He has worked hard all his life to become what he is today and he's proud that there's never been a hint of scandal about the bank or any of his employees. He's rather bitter about the men who make their money by dishonest means. I guess that's why he's over-protective with me. He thinks that every man who wants to court me is only interested in his money."

Bolt helped her down from the buggy, glanced back at Tom who had ridden up behind the coach.

"Well, it's been a pleasure meeting you, Valerie, and I'm glad you weren't hurt."

"Oh, you must come in to meet my parents. They will want to thank you for saving my life."

"Maybe another time." Bolt had no desire to confront her over-protective father. He'd been that route before. "Wouldn't want him to think I was after his money." He reached inside the buggy, grabbed the box of meat and started to hand it to Valerie.

"I insist. You too, Tom." She looped her arm through Bolt's, dragged him toward the front door. She let Bolt carry the package of meat.

Tom climbed down from his horse, tied both of the horses to the fancy hitching post that decorated the driveway. He followed Bolt and the girl to the house.

Valerie opened the door of the elegant two-story house, stepped inside the entry hall that was as large as an entire living room.

"Just set the meat down on the table," she said. "Bing will take care of it." She led them on into the entrance of the living room where her parents were sitting. Her mother got up when she saw Valerie and the two strangers, dashed to the doorway. Her father glanced up from his newspaper, gave Bolt and Tom a cold look.

"Valerie! What happened to your dress? It's burned!"

Her father got up then and walked over to them. He glanced down at the scorched dress, brought his eyes back up to Bolt's, waited for an explanation.

"Oh, it was terrible!" Valerie said, tears welling up in her eyes. "Mister Talbott's yardage store caught on fire while I was in there buying some lace. Oh, this is Jared Bolt and Tom Penrod. Bolt and Tom, I'd like you to meet my parents, Faye and Rodney Blair. Bolt saved my life and Tom saved Mister Talbott's life. The smoke got to me and I passed out in the store. If it hadn't been for Bolt ... I wouldn't be here now ..." Her voice cracked as she related the horror of the incident.

Rodney Blair shook Bolt's hand and then Tom's.

"Pleased to meet you," he said warmly. "We owe you a great deal."

"Come in and sit down," said Faye Blair. "Tell us all about it. I'll have Kali Loo fix us some tea."

Bolt could see where Valerie got her beauty. Faye had bright blue eyes, dark hair like her daughter. If she let her hair down instead of wearing it in a matronly bun, she would be able to pass for Valerie's sister instead of her mother. Valerie's father was equally handsome, tall, with clear blue eyes, enough gray hairs at his temples to make him look distinguished.

He observed the signs of wealth in the room. Oriental rugs, expensive, hand-carved furniture, a piano in one corner of the room and a massive china cabinet that held hand-cut crystal and delicate china plates, imported, he was sure. He noticed the Chinese maid, Kali Loo, who hovered at the back of the room waiting for instructions.

"Thanks, but we won't be staying that long," said Bolt. "We just wanted to see that Valerie got home safely. She was pretty shaken up by the fire."

"Surely you will stay long enough for us to get to know you," Faye said. "After all, you just saved our daughter's life." She was just as insistent as Valerie had been before.

"Perhaps you'd rather have brandy," said Valerie's father.

"I really wish we could stay," Bolt said politely. "Maybe another time. It's almost dark out and we really have to get back." He smiled at Valerie, turned to leave.

Rodney Blair dug into his pocket, drew out a wad of bills. He unrolled them, started to peel some of them off.

"At least accept a reward for saving our daughter's life," he said.

"I wouldn't think of it," said Bolt. "I only did what any other person would have done under the circumstances.''

''Not in this town,'' said Rodney Blair drily. ''People here have forgotten what it's like to care about the life of another human being.''

With that remark, Bolt got his first inkling that all was not well in the magic city that he thought was big enough to rise above the clannishness of a small town.

Chapter Three

The sunlight lasted a long time on top of the hill where Valerie Blair lived with her parents. As Bolt and Tom mounted their horses and rode away, they could see the last chip of the sun melt into the distant landscape below them, off to the west. Although Bolt couldn't actually see the ocean from there, he could imagine the sun falling into its waters. The sky was filled with a warm rosy glow after the sun disappeared. Bolt wished he was at the Pelican Point Hotel where he could watch the sunset over the ocean from his hotel room window.

"What in the hell was your big rush?" Tom asked. "I could have enjoyed myself sitting in that fancy house for a spell. Least we could have done was to stay long enough to taste some of that expensive brandy Rodney offered us. Hell, you want me to get some culture, don't you? You ain't gonna get much higher in society than that family, I reckon."

"I want to get back to town and talk to Talbott."

"Why?"

"I want to find out just how that fire got started."

"What difference does it make now? It's over and done with. Nobody died in the fire."

"No, but there's something funny going on. Besides Talbott and Valerie, the only other person inside the yardage store when the fire started was that man with the limp. I know you were too busy feeding your face to notice him go in the store, but the same man was hanging around Valerie's buggy when I came out of the meat market. I just want to find out how the fire started."

"You still think he's a suspicious character, don't you?"

"Yep."

"Well, if you don't need my help, I think I'll take in a little of the local night life."

"Just so you're up and about early in the morning. I want to look the town over in the light of day. See if we can find a good location for a bawdy house."

"I can check out some of the competition tonight," Tom grinned.

"I figured you would."

As they rode down from the hilltop, they saw the lights of the city begin to come on. By the time they reached the streets of town, the last light of day faded from the sky. The two men parted company to pursue their own interests.

Bolt followed the directions Valerie had given him to get to Talbott's home which was three blocks away from the yardage shop. When he knocked on the door, he was greeted by Talbott's wife. She was an older lady, short and pleasantly plump, gray hair, a friendly face with clear blue eyes.

"You Missus Talbott?" Bolt said.

"Yes." She held the door open just a crack, peeked out at Bolt with a puzzled expression.

"My name's Bolt. I . . ."

"Oh, Mister Bolt! You and your friend helped my husband and that Blair girl. It's so nice to meet you. Please come in." She opened the door wider.

"I just came by to see how your husband is doing."

"I'm terribly worried about him," she whispered. "Maybe you can cheer him up."

"Is he in a lot of pain?"

"Not so much that. Henry's depressed. Losing his business like that at his age isn't easy. We lost everything and we don't have the money to rebuild or even to restock. He bought only the best fabrics he could. He says that there's no use living anymore. I'm so afraid he's going to take his life. Maybe you could say something to him that could change his mind."

She led him to the modest living room which was at the back of the house. Henry Talbott sat on the couch, his left arm loosely bandaged.

"Mister Bolt came by to see how you were doing, Henry," Mrs. Talbott said, trying to hide the hurt in her eyes.

"I'm glad you came, Mister Bolt. I wanted to thank you and Mister Penrod for helping me out."

"Just call me Bolt. How's your arm?"

"Not too bad. Doc Swenson put some ointment on it. If it hadn't been for you and your friend, I reckon Valerie and I would both be goners now. I heard you got her out safe. Thank God you happened along when you did. I tried to get her out. I really did." Tears came to his eyes.

31

"I know you did."

"She was on the other side of the room, toward the back of the store. I couldn't even see her through the smoke, but I knew she was lookin' at the lace back there. Said she was making herself a dress for the big debutante party tomorrow night and she'll be the prettiest debutante there. I ran toward her but when my clothes caught on fire, I . . . I just . . ."

"You did the only thing you could. What about the man who was in your shop? Who was he?"

"Never saw him before, but that don't mean anything. Most of my customers are women. But I can tell you this. If it hadn't been for that rotten lout, there wouldn't have been no fire."

"Oh?"

"He acted kinda funny when he came in. Looked all around like he was looking to see if anyone else was in the store. I thought he was going to rob me. But then he stepped up real close to me and asked where the girl was. I knew then he meant Valerie but I didn't know why he was asking for her. I didn't like the looks of him so I didn't answer him. He asked again and shoved me back against the counter. That's when the lantern fell off the counter and set fire to the bolt of fabric. The fire spread fast through all that material around us. The stranger got scared and made a beeline for the back door. Thank God Valerie was hidden behind the rows of fabric bolts so he couldn't see her. I'm glad she wasn't hurt in the fire."

"I'm glad you weren't hurt worse than you were," Bolt smiled.

"Don't matter much about me. I'm too old to start

32

all over again. But I don't mind. I've had a good life and a good woman. It doesn't matter if I live or die now." He reached his hand up and took his wife's hand in his.

"Don't talk that way, Henry," Marie said, fighting back the tears.

"You still got a good woman," Bolt said, "and a lot of customers who depend on you, I would imagine. You take it easy while that arm of yours heals up and I'll bet by the time you're ready to work again, you'll find a way."

"But I ..."

"Your wife is going to take care of you for a few days. Women love that sort of thing. She'll probably spoil you, but enjoy it while you can. If I had such a pretty woman to take care of me, I'd get married in a minute."

Henry looked up at his wife.

"She is pretty, isn't she?" he smiled.

"Darned right. Now, you take care. I'll check with you later."

"Won't you stay for pie and coffee?" Mrs. Talbott asked. "I was just about to fix some for Henry."

"No thanks," said Bolt. He turned to leave.

Marie followed him to the front door. Impulsively, she stood up on tiptoes, kissed Bolt on the cheek. "Thanks for everything. I know he'll be all right now."

"You both will," Bolt smiled. As she closed the door behind him, he walked back out to his horse, mounted Nick and headed for the Hilltop Restaurant to pay his bill for the supper he and Tom had eaten just before the fire broke out.

The head waiter at the Hilltop House Restaurant, Nicholus Rementi, recognized Bolt when he stepped up to the counter. He looked at Bolt and smiled.

"Hope you didn't think I was skipping out without paying my bill," Bolt said as he took his wallet out of his pocket.

"Wasn't worried a bit, Mister Bolt. What you did to save that girl and that old man showed a lot of courage. Everyone's talking about you."

"How much do I owe you?" Bolt smiled politely.

"Not a thing," Rementi grinned. "It was our pleasure to serve you."

Bolt drew a ten-dollar bill out of his wallet and handed it to the waiter.

"Thanks anyway, but I pay my bills. Keep the change."

"Thank you. By the way, Mister Bolt, there was a girl in here looking for you."

"Oh?" Bolt's brow knotted in puzzlement. He didn't think Valerie Blair had ridden back into town and yet she was the only one he knew in San Francisco.

"Wouldn't give her name, but she's in the small back dining area off the main dining room." Rementi gestured toward the back. "Just go through those curtains."

Bolt turned and walked through the main dining room which was almost full of customers. He observed the diners as he headed toward the long strings of colorful beads that served as a curtain between the main room and the small intimate dining area beyond. The beads rattled as he pulled the strings apart and looked inside the small room that was lit only by a single candle on the table. He saw the girl sitting at the table, her shoulders hunched forward, her head lowered over her tightly clenched hands. She wore a dark shawl draped around her shoulders.

Her head jerked up when she heard the beads rattle. She glanced up at Bolt, her chin resting on her clutched hands. Matted strands of light brown hair hung around her thin pinched face. In the flickering candlelight, Bolt saw the fear in her dark hazel eyes.

"You looking for me?" Bolt said to the girl who almost looked like a witch in the dark shadowy setting.

"Are you Bolt?" Her voice was shaky and no louder than a whisper.

"Yes." Bolt stepped closer, looked down at the girl. He saw that one of her eyes was puffy. The flesh beneath her eye was bruised and purple.

"I heard how you saved that Miss Blair this afternoon."

"Is Valerie a friend of yours?" Bolt pulled out a chair and sat near the frightened girl.

"No. I don't know her. I don't know anyone in town. I was hoping you ... hoping that you could help me."

"What's the matter?"

The girl's eyes darted toward the beaded curtain.

"I can't talk here. Someone might hear me."

"Who hit you?"

"Please ... can we go someplace where we can talk?"

"Where are you staying?"

"That's just it," she said, looking up into Bolt's eyes, "I don't have any place to stay. I don't have any money."

The beads rattled just then. Bolt's eyes shot up to the curtain a few feet away. The strings of beads rippled as if a stick had been drawn across them but he could not see who had looked into the small room. He jumped up, dashed to the curtains and pulled them apart, scanned the big dining room. Only the customers who had been there before were in the room, but several of them had their heads turned, looking toward the lobby as if someone had just dashed by them. The beads tinkled as he let go of the curtain and turned back to the girl. He glanced around, saw a door behind him.

"Come on. Let's get out of here," he whispered. He grabbed the girl's arm, pulled her up out of her chair and pushed her toward the door, hoping that it led to the outside. He opened the door, stepped into darkness. He eased the door closed behind them then realized that they were not outside, but in another room which was pitch dark. He quickly dug in his pocket, drew out a sulphur match, struck it on his denims. When he held the match up in the air, the tiny flame threw a dim light across hulks of boxes and crates, shelves of canned goods and full flour and sugar sacks. Just before the flame sputtered out, he saw the dim outline of another door at the back of the storeroom. Plunged into total darkness again, he held the girl's arm firmly, inched his way across the room, feeling his way by sticking each foot in turn out in front of him. He stubbed his toe twice before he reached the other door.

He struck another match, unbolted the latches across the door. When he tried the door knob, he found it locked. He lit a third match, looked around until he found a tray of big spoons. He grabbed one of the spoons, pried the leather hinges loose from the door. He tugged on the door until it opened enough for them to slide through.

The cool evening breeze brushed against his face as they stepped out into the dark alley behind the restaurant. The only light came from the rising moon, but it was enough for Bolt to check the alley to make sure nobody was watching them. He took the girl's arm again, led her down the dark alley until they came to a cross street. Again, he checked both ways, then crossed the street and continued down another alley that ran between the back sides of the buildings of the busy business district.

He began reading the crude, hand-painted signs that hung over the back doors of the various buildings, finally spotted one that announced the back entrance to the Barbary Hotel. He opened the door, drew the girl inside the lantern-lit hallway, closed the door, then took a deep breath. He didn't think they had been followed and figured this would be a good place for the girl to hide out, if that was what she wanted.

He didn't know who they were running from, but he was sure that whoever had peeked into that intimate dining room meant trouble for the girl. She was badly frightened and obviously bruised. He didn't even know her name, but she needed someone to talk to and a place to stay. He didn't know that he could help her, but he would get her a room for the

37

night and listen to her story.

Suddenly, the humor of the situation hit Bolt. He chuckled to himself. Tom Penrod was right. Tom had said it a hundred times. *Bolt, you're a soft touch for a damsel in distress. Why not pay for a woman's pleasures and be done with it instead of getting involved?* But Bolt figured different. He refused to pay for a woman's charms when most women could be had for nothing. He always told Tom that there was no challenge to plunking down good money in a whorehouse and getting laid by a professional.

He was glad Tom couldn't see him now. Tom would rag his ass a long time about this particular incident.

Chapter Four

Bolt saw the girl's face in the brighter light of the lantern in the hall. He was startled to see that she wore bright smudges of rouge on her cheeks, ruby red lipstick splashed across her lips so they lost their own definition and light pink powder caked on the rest of her face so that she looked like a painted clown. The traditional gaudy makeup that prostitutes wore.

Things were beginning to make sense to him now. He'd seen it happen before. A girl took up the profession of prostitution because she thought it would be exciting and glamorous and then the first time she got a tough customer who roughed her up a bit, she ran scared. He couldn't blame the girl, of course, but if this was the case, he wouldn't be much help to her. If she had chosen that profession, then it was her problem to solve. All he could do was see that she had a safe room for the night.

"Do you want to wait here while I get you a room?" he asked.

"I don't want to go up to the lobby, but I don't

39

want to wait here either," she said, her eyes darting around nervously.

Bolt's boots clanked on the wooden floor as he walked down the hall toward the lobby of the shabby hotel. The girl trotted along behind him, her button-top shoes clicking against the floor. She stopped at the end of the hall, just before they reached the lobby. Around the corner, in the lobby, Bolt found the registration desk. He asked the desk clerk for a room for one person for one night. After Bolt had signed the register with his own name, the clerk handed him a key to the room.

"Room two sixteen," said the bored desk clerk. "You can use the back stairs. First door to your left."

When Bolt reached the hallway again, the girl followed him along the hall, up the stairs. She waited while he opened the door, then stepped inside the small room, closed the door after he lit the lamp.

"You feel better now?" Bolt asked.

"A little. But I need your help."

"I don't even know your name," Bolt smiled.

"Penny. Penelope, actually, but my friends call me Penny."

"You got a last name?"

"Just Penny." She walked over to the bed, sat down on the edge of it, let the dark shawl fall from her shoulders.

Bolt noticed that although she wore a long, dark, heavy skirt, her bodice was bright red, skimpy, barely covered her large breasts that were forced to jut up and out by the stays in the clinging bodice.

"You a prostitute, Penny?" he asked, a casual tone to his voice.

"No. That is, not until today. I mean ..."

"You got yourself into a situation you couldn't handle, and you changed your mind."

"No! It isn't like that at all. I was forced into being a prostitute. I was kidnapped! I've been on a boat for three or four days. I don't even know what day it is. We just arrived this afternoon. In fact, I didn't even know what city I was in until I asked at the restaurant."

His interest perked up, Bolt looked directly at her.

"You say you came by boat?"

"Yes. It was terrible. I was seasick the whole time."

"Were the other girls besides yourself?"

"Yes. About fifteen of us. And four Chinese boys that I saw who had been kidnapped."

"Were you transferred from one boat to another when you arrived?"

"Yes. They put some of us on a smaller boat and took us to shore. How did you know?"

"I think I saw the boats today when they made the transfer, but I didn't know what was going on. Where are you from?"

"Los Angeles. My family is very prominent there. I have to get back to them, but I don't want them to know ... to know what I was forced to do."

"Who kidnapped you?"

"Some big ugly brute. He delivered me to the big boat where the other girls were already aboard. They wouldn't allow us to talk to each other so I didn't find out much about the other girls, but I do know that they were kidnapped too. I found that much out."

"Where did they take you when you got here?"

41

"To a . . . a whorehouse?"

"Which one? Where?"

"I don't know. I don't know!" she cried. "They blindfolded us when they took us off the small boat and loaded us into a covered wagon. It seemed like it took hours before we got anywhere. They didn't take my blindfold off until I was inside that room at the bordello."

"How do you know for sure it was a whorehouse?"

"I didn't know at first. Until a man came into the room and demanded certain things of me. When I refused, he got mad and asked me what I was doing in a whorehouse if I wasn't willing to spread my legs for him. He said he had paid good money for my body, fifty dollars, and he was damned sure going to get his money's worth. He started to knock me around and I was so scared I gave in to him."

"That how you got your black eye?"

"No. It was later. I guess the filthy beast who had his way with me complained to the owner of the bordello because a few minutes after he left, another man came in and slapped me around. Told me I was to do anything the customers wanted. One of his blows caught me across the eye." She buried her head in her hands. "I don't want to talk about it anymore."

"If I'm going to help you, I've got to know these things. How did you get away from there?"

"They blindfolded me again and told me they were going to take me to service a client at his home. Only they didn't use such polite words. That man was worse than the first man. He made me do terrible things to him. When he was through with me he left

42

the room and I sneaked out of the house. He lived a couple of blocks away from the restaurant and I wandered around until I found the restaurant. I went in there to see if I could get something to eat. That's when I heard about the fire and how you had saved the Blair girl. I knew if I could find you, you could help me, too. I knew I could trust you."

"Do you know the names of any of the people involved in kidnapping these girls?"

"No. I never heard any names mentioned. I didn't even see the man who ran the bordello. The man who roughed me up was just a hired strong-arm, I'm sure. He said if I behaved myself and did as I was told, I would be given a free run of the house. Otherwise, I would be kept locked up in my room and not allowed to talk to the other girls. But he never mentioned any names."

"Think hard. It's important."

Penny closed her eyes and lowered her head, ran her fingers across her forehead.

"Yes, I remember one name. When we were transferred to the smaller boat, the captain of the sailing ship told the oarsman of the other boat to take us to shore and to hurry because Jubal was waiting. I didn't know what Jubal was, but it might be a man's name." She got up, walked across the room, poured water from the pitcher into the porcelain bowl. She took a washcloth from the dresser, dipped it into the water, applied soap to the washcloth, then began scrubbing the rouge and powder from her face.

"Not much to go on, but it might help." Bolt stared down at the floor, wondering if Penny's kidnapping had anything to do with Valerie. Probably not, since Penny was brought north by boat from Los Angeles, and Valerie was a local girl. He couldn't make any connection between the two incidents.

Penny rinsed her face, dried it, picked up a hair brush from the dresser. As she began brushing the tangles from her long light brown hair, she turned around to face Bolt.

"I hope so," she said.

Her words broke Bolt's concentration and it took a minute before he knew what she was referring to. When he glanced up at her, he was startled by her beautiful face, the natural beauty that had been hidden by the makeup.

"You're much prettier without all that gook on your face," he smiled.

The brush still in her hand, she ran over to Bolt, threw her arms around his neck.

"Oh, Bolt, I'm so scared. Can you help me to get back home before they find me? I know they'll do horrible things to me if they find me."

Bolt felt her warm body cling to his as she held him tight. She smelled of soap with only a trace of heavy perfume lingering on her clothing.

"We'll find a way," he said, holding her tight. "I'll check to see if there's a stage going south in the morning. If not, we can hire someone to take you home."

"I wish you could take me, Bolt. It's such a long trip and I feel safe with you."

"You'll be safe once we get you out of the city."

"Will you at least spend the night with me? I don't want to be by myself."

Bolt hesitated.

She backed away, hung her head.

"You think I'm dirty and used because I was forced to sleep with those men, don't you? I was a virgin until then."

"It isn't that . . ."

"Bolt, will you make love to me? I need to know what it's like to be with a gentle man."

"What makes you think I'd be gentle?"

"I just know." She threw her arms around his neck again, kissed him hard on the lips. She pressed her body into his, ground her loins against his crotch.

Bolt felt the heat surge into his manhood as it began to expand and stiffen. He felt her breasts crush and flatten into firm lumps against his chest. Her mouth was hot and damp on his lips, searching with a frantic urgency. She tugged at the back of his neck, pulled him toward the bed.

It took her only seconds to get out of her scant clothes and climb in the bed. By the time Bolt stripped out of his clothes and hung his gunbelt on the bedpost, he was fully hard, his cock pulsating with desire.

He crawled into bed beside her, took a breast in his hand and massaged the smooth flesh that yielded to his touch. He kissed her passionately, sliding his rigid tongue inside her warm mouth. She responded, thrust her loins up in the air. Bolt moved his hand down her body, found the furry patch that hid the entrance to her sex. He traced a finger around the nest, found the fleshy lips that begged to be penetrated. She spread her legs, thrust her loins up to meet his hand.

"I want you inside me," she husked. "Now." Her breath was hot on his ear.

Bolt moved over her, straddled her wide-spread legs, his shaft like a stiff arrow aimed at her honey-pot. He reached down and splayed her pussy lips open, lowered himself until the mushroom head of his manhood touched her hot pink lips that were wet and slick with the juices of desire. When he pushed inside her, he felt her tense and tighten. She gasped, cried out.

"Did I hurt you?" Bolt asked.

"No! No! It feels so good. You're so big. I want you all the way inside me. Deeeeeep inside me."

Bolt plunged in deep, felt her damp folds tighten around him, hold him there where it was warm and wonderful.

"Oh, yes, yes, yes," she panted, her body bucking and undulating beneath him. "You make me feel so good. So tingly. I've never known such exquisite pleasure."

Bolt plunged deeper and deeper with each stroke, unable to slow himself down. He had been a long time without a woman and Penny's bucking body drove him to the brink of ecstasy. He pumped into her, felt his seed begin to boil. He pushed into her with one final thrust, jamming his cock to the hilt as his seed bubbled over into her folds in short spurts.

"I can't believe how good it was," she said when he rolled off her. "I wouldn't mind being a prostitute if all the men was as good as you are."

"Thanks."

"I feel so weak. I don't have the strength to get up."

"Did you eat at the restaurant, Penny?"

"No. I didn't get a chance before you got there

although the waiter said he would get me something and I could pay him later."

"How long has it been since you've eaten?"

"I don't know. Days. I tried to eat when I was on the boat but I couldn't keep anything down."

"I'm going to go find you something to eat. Maybe they have a dining room in the hotel. If not, I'm sure there's a cafe nearby. I won't be gone long." Bolt got up, dressed, buckled his gunbelt around his waist.

"When you get back, will you spend the night with me?"

"Yes, I will."

Outside the hotel room, a man stood right next to the door. He had been looking for Penny all evening, ever since he found out that she had escaped from Mayor Kallock's home after the mayor had finished with her.

The man pressed his ear to the door, smiled when he recognized the girl's voice. He had found the girl once tonight. In the back room of the restaurant. When he had peeked in the beaded curtains, he had seen that she was with a man who had glanced up when the curtains rattled. Not wanting to be spotted, he had fled from the restaurant, waited outside so he could follow the girl when she came out. When he realized that she and the man had sneaked out the back way, his search started all over again. He had gone to three different hotels, asking if someone had checked in within the last half hour, before he had come here a few minutes ago. He had arrived just in time to hear the stranger pouring the meat to Penny. He wondered who the stranger was, if Penny had

47

spilled her guts to the man. It wouldn't go over very well with his boss, the Chinaman, if any of their secrets got out. He wished he knew who the stranger was.

When he heard the stranger say he was going out for food for Penny, the man outside the door backed away, tiptoed down the hall, disappeared around the corner. This was the break he was looking for.

It took Bolt a little over a half an hour to scramble up some food for Penny from a nearby restaurant. He knew she would need her strength for the long trip to Los Angeles if he could arrange transportation for her early in the morning.

When he got back to the room at the Barbary Hotel, he knocked lightly on the door, called out his name so he wouldn't frighten Penny, then opened the door and stepped inside.

"I got it," he announced, holding the sack of food up for her to see. He looked over at the bed. His heart skipped a beat when he saw that it was empty. He looked around the small room as if he expected her to be there. Then he studied the room carefully, saw no sign of a struggle. Her clothes were gone and so was she. It was that simple.

He waited for more than an hour before he headed back to the Pelican Point Hotel. If she had been kidnapped again, he wouldn't know where to begin looking for her. Chances were, she had changed her mind about going back to Los Angeles and she had just left before he returned. Maybe she had made the whole story up.

Back in his room at the Pelican Point, Bolt stood at

48

the open window for a long time before he went to bed. The moon, which was almost full, deposited a silver path across the ocean waters.

He wondered what had happened to Penny. He believed her story about being kidnapped. He had seen the boats offshore. But he had no clues to her disappearance except the name "Jubal." It wasn't much to go on in this big city.

His thoughts shifted to Valerie Blair. She was in danger, too, he knew, but again, his only clue was the man with the limp who had followed her into the fabric shop.

Bolt stared at the green, glimmering phosphorescent waves that pounded the shoreline, hypnotized by their constant crashing thunder. He searched for the answers to his questions in the dark expanse of water below. But the ocean would not give up the answers this night.

Chapter Five

Across town, Jubal Naylor sat in his plush office in the fancy bordello, The House Of Paradise, which he owned. The bordello had earned the reputation as San Francisco's most infamous and high-priced whorehouse. Naylor charged his customers fifty to a hundred dollars for the pleasures of one of his beautiful prostitutes, but none of them complained. The clients he drew to the whorehouse were not only willing to pay his price, they were wealthy enough to afford it and considered it exclusive because they knew men of lesser means could not patronize the bordello and contaminate the lovely girls. In return for the high fees, Naylor assured them of complete discretion and secrecy concerning their visits to the elegant establishment.

Jubal owned the bordello, but none of his clients realized that he was involved in a much larger operation and that the bordello was only a front for the other part of his business. The Chinaman was the big boss of the operation, although Jubal preferred to

"Why didn't you grab her before she went inside? Or was that too hard for you?" Jubal's voice was sarcastic.

"I didn't have no chance to. Too many people around. When the fire started, I couldn't even find her in all that thick smoke. I ran out the back door and was damned lucky just to get out with my skin. I thought for sure she was a goner in that fire but when I went around to the front of the building, I saw this feller carrying her out. I didn't have no chance to get her after that 'cause that feller what rescued her stuck right with her."

"It was a simple job, Gimpy. But I didn't figure you could stay sober long enough to handle it."

"You got me all wrong, Jubal. I ain't been drinkin'. I can get that Blair girl for you, but I want my money up front this time. You promised to pay me half of the fifty dollars before I kidnapped the girl and the other half when I delivered. So far, I ain't seen a damn dime from you."

"You'll get the whole fifty when you deliver."

"I always thought you was good for your word, but I guess that's all changed now that you got yourself a partner. Ain't your boss' style to kidnap a local gal, is it?" Troller paused, let his words sink in.

Jubal's face reddened. He fought the anger that boiled up inside him.

"What the hell are you talking about? You drunk?"

"No. Ain't had a drink in a week. But I know all about you and the Chinaman and all those high-falutin gals you're roundin' up. You know, I been thinkin', Jubal, maybe your boss don't know about

53

that Blair gal. Maybe that was somethin' you cooked up just for yourself.''

Naylor cursed under his breath. Somehow, Gimpy had figured everything out, even about the Blair gal. No, the Chinaman didn't know about her. That was his own idea and he had planned to rent her out to a couple of his special customers for a tidy sum, then hold her for ransom. Let her old man pay through the nose to get her back. There'd even be some hush money in it. Banker Blair wouldn't want his daughter involved in a scandal. He'd pay a handsome fee to get his daughter back alive and to keep her reputation unsoiled. She was worth a bloody fortune.

No, the Chinaman wouldn't like it a bit if he found out Naylor planned to snatch the Blair girl. The other girls were used to generate large sums of money, but never from demanding ransom money. And none of the girls were from the San Francisco area. That was one of the Chinaman's rules. In fact, it was Woo Fong's insistence on leaving the local girls out of the kidnap ring that had given Jubal the idea to steal the Blair girl and keep the profits for himself. He knew he could do it without anyone knowing about it.

Jubal wasn't sure just how much Gimpy knew, but he couldn't risk letting Gimpy blab what he did know to Woo Fong. He'd have to get rid of Gimpy.

Naylor took his hands from his desk, slid them down, eased his top desk drawer open. As he started to reach for the loaded pistol inside the drawer, he had second thoughts. He'd take Gimpy out, but not there at the bordello. Too many questions to answer if he shot him there in the office. It would be easy enough, though. Just give Gimpy enough drinking money and the rest would be a piece of cake.

"Seems I misjudged you, Gimpy," Jubal smiled. "We could use someone smart as you in our operation. Since you figured everything out, you know there's plenty of money to go around. I'll tell the Chinaman we've got a new partner." He drew a stack of bills from the top drawer, held them in his hand.

Troller eyed the money. "You still want me to get that Blair gal?" he grinned.

"Yeah, sure, but there's no hurry. We'll let it go until after the weekend. I'm gonna pay you the twenty-five now and by this time next week, you'll be rolling in money." Jubal counted out the bills, handed them to Gimpy. "Go buy yourself a drink. You deserve it. Come back to see me Monday morning. And buy yourself some new duds before you come back. If you're going to be a part of our company, you'll need to dress the part."

"Thanks, Jubal. I know you won't be sorry." Troller took the money, stuffed it in his jacket pocket.

"Not a word of this to anyone," Jubal cautioned.

"You can trust me," Troller grinned. He turned and walked out of Naylor's plush office, feeling smug about himself because he had bluffed his way into the organization.

After Troller left, Jubal got up from his desk. He knew Gimpy would head straight for his favorite watering hole, Barney's Red Dog Saloon. The bar was on the next street behind the bordello, a short block away. Gimpy was a creature of habit. With money in his pocket, he wouldn't be able to stay away from the booze.

Naylor already had a holstered pistol tucked away

under his expensive suit jacket. But he would use it only as a last resort. It would be too noisy for his purposes. He withdrew a knife from the bottom drawer of his desk, slid it out of its sheath, ran his thumb over the blade to test its sharpness. He slipped the knife back into the sheath, put it in his waistband.

He'd give Gimpy time to enjoy his drinks. They would be the last he'd ever have.

Tom Penrod was awed by the lights of San Francisco at night. Riding the trail with Bolt for so long, there was no way he could have imagined a town this size. He had heard the stories about the social and cultural life in San Francisco, and even riding through the town, he was amazed at the number of theatres and opera houses, the fine restaurants. He could see why Bolt was so fascinated by the town on the Barbary Coast.

After riding through the streets to familiarize himself with the town, he stopped in front of Barney's Red Dog Saloon, dismounted and tied his horse to the rail. Inside the saloon, he found it to be much like any other bar he had visited across the West. Maybe a little larger. But the smell of stale beer and whiskey, cigarette and cigar smoke, was the same. He strolled over to the long bar, ordered a whiskey from the friendly bartender. When the drink was delivered, he drank it slowly, turned to watch the other customers.

"You don't have any glitter gals here?" Tom asked when the bartender stopped in front of him.

"Nope," said the balding bartender. "But there are several places in town that do."

"Any suggestions?" Tom said.

"Depends on what you're looking for. How much you want to spend. Cheapest place is called The Fortune Cookie. At the other end of the scale is the House of Paradise on the next block over from here. I hear it's a good place if you can afford their prices. They offer high-class dames, fifty bucks a half hour, a hundred bucks for anything different, but to me, a pussy's a pussy. The Tradewinds is a decent place. Clean gals, clean sheets and it won't cost you an arm or a leg."

Tom sipped on his drink as the bartender moved away to pour a drink for someone else.

One of the customers staggered by Tom, headed for the door. He was so drunk, his limp was hardly noticeable. Something about the man caught Tom's attention, rang a bell in his mind, but he couldn't think why he should know the man. It wasn't until some ten minutes later when Tom finished his drink that he knew who the man was. It was the short pants, the ill-fitting black jacket the man wore that had triggered Tom's memory. The drunk was the man who had been inside the yardage store when it burned. The one Bolt was suspicious of. Damn, he wished he had recognized him earlier so that he could have followed him. He knew the man would be gone by now.

Tom set his empty glass down on the bar top, turned to leave. He'd go to the Tradewinds, see if the San Francisco girls were any better than the prostitutes in small towns. Outside, he breathed in the cool fresh air, swore he could smell the ocean from there. The boardwalk was well lit by the storm lanterns that hung from posts in front of the saloon. Other businesses along the street that were open that time of night also displayed lanterns of welcome for their customers.

As Tom started to untie the reins from the hitching rail, something at the corner of the building caught his eye. He looked over, saw that someone was sprawled out on the boardwalk in the alley between the saloon and the next building. Only the legs and feet were visible, but he recognized the short pant legs that rode six inches above the man's ankles. At first he thought the man had passed out in the alley. But when he walked over and looked around the corner at the drunk, his stomach turned queasy. The man lay in a pool of blood, his throat cut open like a ripe watermelon.

Tom peered down the dark alley, then looked up and down the street, his eyes scanning the boardwalks for any sign of a man running from the murder scene. He didn't see anyone on the street or in the alley.

Without hesitation, he went back inside the saloon, stood at the end of the bar until the bartender spotted him and walked over to see what he wanted.

"Forget something?" the bartender smiled.

"You know that drunk who staggered out of here about ten or fifteen minutes ago?" Tom said in a hushed voice.

"You talkin' about Gimpy? Yeah. He can really tie one on when he's got money in his pocket."

"Well, his drinkin' days are over. Somebody snuffed him in the alley."

"Damn! Poor Gimpy. A born loser. A drunk, but he never hurt anybody in his life, far as I know. He was

58

flashing a wad of bills in here tonight. Playing the bigshot. Buying drinks for everyone. Somebody must have rolled him for his money."

"Where'd he get his money?" Tom asked. "Who'd he work for?"

"Never knew about Gimpy. Most of the time he was broker than a squashed egg. Think he earned his pocket money by doing odd jobs for anybody who'd hire him. He must have scored big this time. Never saw him with so much money. He must've had fifty bucks on him." The bartender came around the end of the bar, followed Tom outside.

"It's pretty gruesome," Tom warned.

The bartender took one look at Gimpy's bloody slit throat, then gagged and turned away. "Oh, my God. Whoever did this must have been pretty damn desperate for money. Did you see anyone out here?"

"No. I was over there untying my horse when I saw his legs sticking out. I thought he'd passed out until . . ."

The bartender shook his head, walked back toward the door of the saloon. "I'll send for the sheriff, but chances are they won't find Gimpy's murderer. They don't concern themselves too much when drunks get killed."

Tom turned and walked back to his horse. He thought about riding back to his hotel to tell Bolt about the man with the limp, but it could wait. Right now, more than before, he needed the affection and attention of a woman.

Chapter Six

Bolt was shaving when Tom knocked on his door the next morning. He had slept soundly to the constant crash of waves against the shore. Haunting visions of the beautiful Valerie Blair had intruded on his dreams of sailing ships and vast ocean waters. Feeling totally refreshed, Bolt went to the door, spatters of shaving lather on his face, a towel draped across his shoulder.

"You're up early," Bolt said when he opened the door. "Or are you just getting home?"

"I was home by midnight. Didn't hear any signs of life over here so I figured you went calling on Miss Blair again."

Bolt walked back to the dressing table, wiped the lather from his face, looked in the mirror.

"No. She's a little out of my league. Her father's too damned strict about the men who court her. I doubt if I'll ever see her again."

"She'll probably end up marrying some socially proper asshole and spend the rest of her days bored to tears."

"What a waste, but it's not my problem." Bolt picked up a comb and combed his hair, decided he needed a haircut. "I just think she's in some kind of danger, but I guess that's not my problem either."

"You talkin' about that man with the limp?"

"Yeah. I'm still wondering why he followed Valerie into that yardage store. He caused the fire when he pushed old man Talbott out of his way. He was definitely looking for Valerie and yet she said she didn't know him."

"Well, you can stop worrying about him. Gimpy was killed last night outside the Red Dog Saloon where I was having a drink. Throat slit from ear to ear."

"Oh?" Bolt turned and looked at Tom who was standing at the window staring at the ocean.

"The barkeep said Gimpy was a loser. A drunk. He said nobody would care much about Gimpy's death. Guess Gimpy did odd jobs to earn his drinking money, but other than that he wasn't much use to society. The barkeep thinks someone rolled him for his money because he was flashing a wad of bills in the bar."

"A drunk. A loser. And yet he had money last night. Wonder who he was working for to get that money and whether it had anything to do with Valerie."

"I reckon you'll never know. He's gone and the barkeep said the sheriff would chalk it up to a drunk being rolled for his money. Probably killed by another drunk who needed money for booze."

"I guess I'll never know the whole story. I just hope to hell that Valerie's not in any trouble. Oh, you know those boats we saw yesterday, the ones with the girls on board?"

"Yair."

"Well, I ran into a girl named Penny last night who claimed she had been kidnapped in Los Angeles and brought here by boat to work in a whorehouse. She said she wanted me to help her get back to her home down south."

"What happened?"

"Damned if I know. I went out to get her something to eat because she said she hadn't eaten in days and when I got back, she was gone."

"Sounds far-fetched to me."

"We did see the boats. I didn't make that up."

"You do get yourself into trouble over women."

"It's what makes life interesting. Let me get a clean shirt on and we'll ride into the big city and look it over."

"It's quite a town. But your idea of opening a classy bawdy house in San Francisco isn't exactly original. There's one here that charges fifty to a hundred bucks for a quick lay. The House of Paradise."

"I said I wanted to open a classy whorehouse here, not an expensive one. You go there?"

"Hell, no. I ain't gonna spend that kind of money on a woman."

"I don't know why you spend any money at all with all the free stuff walking around just begging to be laid. You wouldn't find me paying for it."

"You pay for it, all right. You just do it in a different way. Besides, I don't like to get involved with a woman the way you do. I'm not the type to go courting with a box of chocolates tucked under my arm and a bouquet of posies clutched in my hands."

"You sure as hell aren't," Bolt laughed. "You're like a rabbit. You hop on, squeal and hop off and it's all over with. Where's the challenge in that?"

"Between their legs. Someday you're gonna realize it's better my way. The women you get involved with always lead you straight into trouble and you end up with someone trying to shoot your ass off."

"Not true, Tom." Bolt buttoned his clean shirt, fastened his gunbelt around his waist.

"Want me to name them? Brenda Wilkins. You got caught in the sack with her by her angry husband and he almost blew your balls off. Have you forgotten? And what about Amylou Lovett? Hell, you get robbed by three thugs while you're balling her. Then there's Rawhide Kate who . . ."

"What are you doing, writing a book about the subject?"

"Would make interesting reading."

"Come on. Let's ride into town and get something to eat. Then we can start looking for a good place for our new bawdy house."

Bolt walked over to the door. Just as he reached for the door knob, someone knocked.

"You expecting anyone, Tom?"

"Nope."

Bolt opened the door, recognized the man who stood before him. It was Bing Chee, the Chinese servant who worked for the Blair family.

"Mister Blair asked me to deliver this to both of you." He handed Bolt a large white envelope. On the outside of the envelope, written in flowing script, were Bolt's and Tom's names.

Bolt tore the envelope open, pulled out a white printed card. He glanced at it, then read it aloud. "The honor of your presence is requested at the San Francisco Starlight Society Debutante Ball, to be held the evening on March 2nd, 1879, at the Shorecliff Club. The following young ladies will be presented during the Grand Ball. Miss Valerie Blair, Miss Jane Ellington, Miss Annabelle Snyder, Miss Rebecca Reynolds and Miss Heather Alexander. Formal attire required. R.S.V.P." When he was finished reading the invitation, Bolt glanced at Tom, saw the silly smirk on his face. "March second. That's tonight, isn't it?"

"You will come?" Bing Chee grinned, his white teeth glistening. He waited for Bolt's reply.

"Tell Mister Blair thank you for the invitation and that we regret that we will not be able to attend his daughter's coming-out party."

"Why not?" Tom snorted. "That's a chance of a lifetime. Why pass it up?"

"I don't dance," Bolt said.

Bing's face became serious. "Miss Valerie insists you come to her party. Missus Blair, too. It would be an insult to turn Mister Blair down. To refuse him is to refuse to let him show his gratitude to you."

"Looks like we're forced to go," Tom grinned.

"Tom, you got anything to wear besides those dusty denims and those old scuffed boots?"

"No, but ..."

"There's your answer. Sorry, Bing Chee. We don't have the proper clothes to attend the party."

"Mister Blair, he tell me to tell you to go to the

Penguin Tuxedo Shop where you can rent the black suits. Shoes, too. He say to charge it to his account.''

"They're very persistent, aren't they?" Bolt laughed.

"Yes, insistent."

"Okay. We'll go. But we'll pay for our own suits."

"Mister Blair say he will send a carriage for you at eight o'clock tonight."

"No, Bing Chee. We will get there on our own."

"Very well. I tell him." Bing Chee nodded his head, then turned and walked away.

"You should have accepted the buggy ride," Tom said after Bing Chee was gone. "It would have been fun."

"No thanks. I don't want to be trapped there. If I don't like the way things are going, I want to be able to leave without waiting for a carriage."

"What makes you think you won't like it?"

"Society people tend to be stuffy. Besides, I don't like crowds and I sure as hell don't know much about ballroom dancing."

"That's it, isn't it, Bolt? You're afraid you're gonna end up a wallflower. Or you'll try to dance and ruin your image."

"No, it'll be fun to see how the other half lives. We've got a lot to do before tonight so let's get to it."

The Shorecliff Club sat on a high cliff overlooking the ocean, not too far from the Pelican Point Hotel. The main two-story building housed a grand ball-room, a large meeting hall for its members, several smaller meeting rooms, a kitchen that was large enough to handle food for more than five hundred people at a time and an elegant entrance lobby that was bigger than most houses. The upstairs rooms were sometimes used by the employees who were needed to run the club when they had elaborate affairs such as the one that night. The groundskeeper and his wife lived in a small cottage next to the mansion.

Nestled in the pines and twisted cypress trees out behind the main building were a dozen individual bungalows that were available for visiting dignitaries or club members who wanted to use them for a time of solitude. Flowers that thrived in the damp ocean air were abundant throughout the neatly manicured grounds. On the far corner of the estate, a dozen horses were kept in the riding stables for use by members.

Bolt and Tom arrived at the Shorecliff Club riding their own horses. Bolt felt awkward wearing the black tuxedo while he was in the saddle. He preferred the casual cowboy clothes he normally wore.

Glimmering hurricane lanterns bordered the path leading up to the private estate and the front of the white mansion glistened in the light of similar lamps. Stylish buggies pulled by sleek, groomed horses, were lined up at the entrance of the building, dispensing elegantly dressed women and men in crisp black suits. Bolt eased his horse around the line of buggies, found the cleared area beyond the entrance where other buggies were already parked for the duration of the ball. The parking area was lit by more than twenty hurricane lanterns that dangled from posts.

"Good evening, Mister Bolt, Mister Penrod. Miss

Blair will be velly happy you come to the Ball."

Bolt looked up from the hitching post to see Bing Chee walking toward him from the Blair horse and buggy which was already parked.

"Evening, Bing Chee. Don't know that I'll stay very long. I don't like mobs." Bolt brushed the dust from his black trousers.

"All nice people. You like them."

"Easy for you to say. You don't have to go in there with all those strangers." The three men walked toward the mansion together. Bing Chee was dressed in his traditional uniform, but it was obviously brand new.

"No," Bing Chee grinned, "tonight we have our own party. If you need me, I be in the back room next to the kitchen."

"You'll probably have more fun than we will."

"Maybe so. The bosses give us servants a special party tonight. Good food. Drinks. We kick up our heels."

"I know where I can go if I get bored," Bolt laughed. "Have fun, Bing Chee."

"You are most welcome at my party," Bing Chee said as he left them at the bottom of the stairs. He would use the back entrance as would the other servants who were there.

"Well, I'm going to have a good time," Tom said as he adjusted the lapels of his black jacket. "Just think of all those sweet, young, high-class pussies in there just itching to be diddled."

"I prefer my sex a little more private, if you don't mind," Bolt grumbled. "Now if you'll quit drooling all over yourself, we can go in and get it over with."

"Don't hurt to look. Come on, Bolt, relax and enjoy yourself," Tom said as they walked up the wide steps. "It ain't gonna kill you to spend a couple of hours with these people."

Bolt stretched his neck, hooked a finger inside the stiff, starched collar of his white shirt, pulled it away from his neck.

"I won't relax until I get out of this damned monkey suit."

Chapter Seven

A doorman dressed in a snappy uniform, black trousers and burgundy-colored jacket, opened the heavy hand-carved door for Bolt and Tom when they reached the top of the steps.

As Bolt stepped inside the large foyer, he heard the strains of the orchestra that filtered from the ballroom, the overtone of voices as people greeted each other. The scent of burning incense was pleasant, not overpowering. Baskets of bright flowers adorned the room while delicate bouquets rested in cut crystal vases on marble tables.

Bolt's polished black shoes made no noise as he walked across the plush Oriental rug, following the other guests into the massive ballroom. Shortly after they entered the festive room, Rodney Blair approached them.

"So glad you could make it," Blair said as he shook hands with both of them. He escorted them over to the side of the room where his wife was standing with two other couples.

Faye Blair looked even more like her daughter than she had before with her dark hair swept back from her face. She wore a peach colored gown that emphasized her slim figure, expensive pearl necklace and earrings, a matching bracelet. Bolt noticed the way her deep blue eyes traveled up and down his form, then settled on his eyes.

"You're looking very handsome tonight," she said, offering the remark to both Bolt and Tom. She held her hand out to Bolt, continued to stare at him.

"And you look lovely." Bolt took her hand, brought it up, brushed it with his lips. He didn't know why he did it. It just seemed like the thing to do. Uncomfortable under her penetrating gaze, he shifted his weight from one foot to the other, cleared his throat. He looked away from her, scanned the room.

"Where's Valerie?"

"She's upstairs with the other debutantes, getting ready for her big moment. It'll be about a half an hour before they make their grand entrance, over there." She pointed to the wooden archway in front of the stage where the orchestra was playing. Masses of flowers adorned the archway where the girls would appear, one at a time, to be presented to the gathering of San Francisco's most elite and influential society men and women.

"Jared Bolt and Tom Penrod," Rodney interrupted, "I'd like you to meet some friends of mine. Joseph Snyder and his lovely wife, Catherine. Their daughter, Annabelle is one of the debutantes. And this is Emory Howes, long time friend and vice-president of my bank. His charming wife, Margaret."

"Pleased to meet you," Howes said, pumping

70

Bolt's hand. He was about six inches shorter than any of the other men in the group so he had to look up to Bolt. "These must be the gentlemen you told me about, Rodney."

"Yes. Bolt was the one who risked his own life to go inside that burning building to save my Valerie. And Penrod helped Talbott when the old man was a human torch. Brave souls."

"Indeed!" said Emory, stroking his bearded chin as he studied the two men. "We're mighty proud to have both of you here tonight as our distinguished guests. You are true heroes."

"You make too much out of it. We just happened to see the smoke and we were able to get there in time to help." Bolt smiled politely. There was something about Howes that bothered Bolt. Howes wore a tuxedo like everyone else, but on him it didn't look natural. Maybe it was because he was shorter than the others. His hair seemed unruly, too, but it wasn't his appearance that was annoying, Bolt decided. The man came on too strong, too aggressive, maybe, like he was trying to prove to everyone that he was a good fellow. A "people pleaser." That's what Bolt called a man like that. Howes seemed over-confident of himself. Not like Rodney Blair who was completely comfortable with himself and his surroundings.

"Nonsense," said Howes. "You really are heroes. I know there are some important people here who would like to meet you. Come on, I'll introduce you."

"We're just visitors, Mister Howes," Bolt said. "Valerie Blair and the other debutantes are the important ones tonight."

"But the Mayor and other people will surely want

to meet you and I'd like to do the honors."

Howes was just about to lead Bolt and Tom away when Faye Blair spoke up. "Maybe you two would like a drink before you meet any more people," she said.

"Good idea," Bolt smiled.

"Yes, by all means, get a drink first," said Emory. "Then I'll introduce you around."

Faye looped her arm through Bolt's arm, nodded for Tom to follow them to the bar that had been set up along the wall on the opposite side of the dance floor.

"Don't mind Emory," she said when they were away from the others. "He's just anxious to show you off."

"Why? We're just a couple of country bumpkins come to the big city. Strangers in town, drifters."

"Don't underestimate yourself, Bolt. Everyone here has heard about your actions in saving our daughter's life. Both of you. But maybe Emory's the one who wants to show off. He's funny that way. He probably figures he can score some points if he is the one to introduce you to the other guests."

"Hero by association," Tom commented.

"Or guilty by association," Bolt smiled.

"Something like that. Would you like a cup of punch or something stronger?" Faye said, gesturing toward the long table that was covered with a lace tablecloth. A crystal punchbowl sat on one end of the table, bottles of expensive whiskey and brandy at the other end.

"Whiskey for me," Bolt said, "Tom?"

"I'll have the same thing?"

The man tending bar stepped forward. He wore the traditional black pants and red uniform jacket that all of the other servants at Shorecliff Club wore. Dangling from a gold chain around his neck was the golden key to the wine cellar. He poured two glasses of whiskey, handed them across the table, then stepped back.

"Just thought I'd warn you that Emory can make a pest of himself at times," said Faye. "He's a nice enough fellow, but he may try to monopolize your time. I feel sorry for him sometimes. He's an old school chum of Rodney's, very popular back then, from what Rodney has told me. In fact, everyone thought Emory Howes would be the most successful graduate of that school. I guess he's still trying to live up to that expectation. But he never made much of himself. A year ago when Rodney's mother was dying, we went back to his hometown in Kansas. That was the first time Rodney had seen Emory in nearly twenty years and it crushed him to see his old friend in such dire straits. Emory was the best man at our wedding, always the life of the party. To make a long story short, Rodney offered to hire him on at the bank and Emory came back to San Francisco with us. Rodney says he's a good employee, but sometimes I wonder. It seems to me that Emory tries too hard to please people and to be accepted into the social circle. People would like him a lot better if he didn't press it so much. But then it's not my place to criticize. We all have our faults. At least he's never been an embarrassment to Rodney or the bank. My husband's a stickler on honesty and integrity, on keeping the reputation of the bank spotless."

"I hope Howes isn't looking to me as some sort of model," Bolt said, " 'cause I reckon I got as many flaws as the next man."

"Maybe he's hoping some of your bravery will rub off on him. I'm going upstairs to check on Valerie. Enjoy yourselves. I'll be back before the girls are presented. Don't forget, they will be serving a buffet supper at midnight. And I wouldn't mind at all if you asked me for a dance." Faye turned and walked away, her peach gown flowing gracefully around her as she sailed across the nearly empty dance floor.

Bolt moved a few feet away from the bar, turned to watch the people in their fancy clothes, their expensive jewels worn like proud badges of their wealth. As the women swished by in their long colorful gowns, escorted by their men in the black tuxedos, Bolt wondered how many of them could measure up to Rodney Blair's strict code of ethics. Not many, he'd bet. Men were men, no matter what their social status. There were bad apples in any class of society and these people were no different. The only thing was, they had more money.

"You can almost smell the money in here, the wealth," he said to Tom. "If you ask me, wealth is wasted on the wealthy, just as youth is wasted on the young."

"Reckon we're in the wrong business?" Tom laughed.

"Nope. I'm perfectly happy being what I am."

"And what might that be?"

"Comfortable with myself. That's all I need out of life." Bolt sipped from his glass as he watched a pretty, young girl walk by. Her breasts, which were as big as large melons, strained against the silk fabric of her tight red gown. As she went by, she turned and smiled coyly at the two men. Bolt smiled politely at her, then turned away. A mild flirtation, but she was much too young to encourage.

"I'll bet that's tight," Tom cracked after the girl was out of earshot.

"Yeah. Known as jail bait where I come from."

"What do you suppose these people would think of us if they knew we ran a string of whorehouses across the country?"

"Hell, we'd probably be the most popular fellows here. People with high morals are always fascinated by the forbidden things in life. Wouldn't surprise me a bit if the majority of the men have spent some time and money in bordellos."

"Right. They're about the only ones wealthy enough to spend a hundred bucks getting their rocks off at that whorehouse I was telling you about. Oh, oh, don't look back, but here comes your friend."

"Who?" Bolt turned to see Emory Howes walking across the dance floor, making a bee-line in their direction.

"Too late to hide," Tom laughed.

Bolt shrugged his shoulders. "Let the poor chap have his moment of glory. If he wants to rub elbows with the likes of us, we'll give him what he's looking for."

"Where do you get this 'we' shit? I think I'll take a powder."

"Chicken," Bolt said.

"If you gentlemen are ready," Howes said as he reached them, "I'll introduce you to some of the key people here. You can carry your drinks with you."

"I was just on my way to take a leak," Tom said. "I'll catch up to you later."

Howes nodded, turned on his heels, motioned for Bolt to follow him back across the dance floor.

Howes stopped several times, introducing Bolt to prominent couples. Each time, he told the story of Bolt's heroic efforts to save the Blair girl, embellishing the fine details. He guided Bolt to the middle of the room where a large, important-looking man was standing, talking with a slender man who was not dressed in a tuxedo.

"And now you're going to meet the most important man in San Francisco," Howes said in a loud exaggerated voice. "Isn't that right, Mayor?"

The tall, broad shouldered man turned around, eyed Bolt suspiciously, a phony politician's smile pasted across his face. "Hello, Emory. How's the world treating you?"

"Can't complain. Mister Bolt, I'd like you to meet the new mayor of San Francisco, Isaac Kalloch."

Kalloch was more than six feet tall with a crop of red hair on his head, a receding hairline. Although he didn't have a moustache, he sported a full, bristly beard that was as red as his hair.

After the men shook hands, Emory told the mayor of Bolt's importance.

"We're honored to have you here," Kalloch said. "Now if you'll excuse me, I'm quite busy. Stamps here is interviewing me for a story in the San Francisco Chronicle. As soon as we're through, I'll be introducing the girls as they make their entrance."

"We understand," said Howes. He turned to the

reporter. "Merle Stamps, this is Mister Bolt. If you'd like to do a story on him, I could arrange it for you."

"I might be interested," Stamps said.

"Come on, Bolt," said Howes, "there's someone else I want you to meet." He dragged Bolt away from the mayor, headed in another direction.

"Hell, I thought I'd met everyone here. Can't it wait till later?"

"Just one more, I promise. This next man is probably the richest man in San Francisco, although very few people know it. He pulls a lot of power around here, but he doesn't brag about it the way the mayor does."

Emory stopped in front of a short, broad-chested Chinaman.

"Good evening, Woo Fong. I'd like you to meet Jared Bolt who is a very special guest here tonight." He went on and gave every small detail of the rescue. Then he spent the next couple of minutes telling Bolt what a nice man Woo Fong was, how much he was respected in the community.

Fong was polite, but reserved, probably as bored with the conversation as Bolt was. Bolt glanced around, spotted the Blairs near the front of the room. Tom had joined them and they seemed to be enjoying themselves, which was more than Bolt could say for himself.

Bolt was relieved when the orchestra began playing again and the mayor announced that the young debutantes were about to make their entrance.

"Time for me to join the Blairs," Bolt said. "I don't want to miss this."

"Yes, go ahead," Emory said as he stepped away from the Chinaman. "But as soon as the girls have made their debut, I'll talk to you again. I have something to show you. I have a surprise for you and Tom that will make your head spin. After the first dance is over with, be prepared for the treat of your life."

Bolt knew that Emory Howes was trying to impress him, but he didn't care to spend any more time with the man. Still, Bolt walked away from Howes, mildly curious about the surprise he had to offer.

Chapter Eight

Valerie Blair looked even more beautiful than Bolt remembered as she walked through the flowered archway beneath the stage when her name was called. Standing near the Blairs, Bolt was close enough to Valerie to see the blue of her eyes, the soft touch of rouge on her face. Her long dark hair was pulled back from her face, fell in soft ringlets from the blue velvet bow that held her hair back. Her gown was a soft blue velvet, full flowing skirt and a form fitting bodice that showed her bustline to advantage, long sleeves that were puffed up at the shoulders.

Bolt knew that Valerie had made her own gown and that the lace she had been looking for was meant for this special occasion. He noticed that instead of the lace, she had used rows of gathered velvet to trim the dress.

Bolt glanced over at Valerie's mother, saw the tears that welled up in her eyes. He knew how proud she was of her daughter.

Valerie beamed when she spotted her parents in

the crowd. When she saw Bolt, her smile widened. She walked the length of the red carpet that had been stretched out across the dance floor, holding a bouquet of roses that Mayor Kalloch had presented to her when she appeared in the archway. When she reached the far end of the room, she turned around, walked back, and took her place between her parents while the other girls were presented. Once she was in position, she turned her head and smiled at Bolt who was standing right behind her with Tom.

None of the other debutantes could match Valerie's natural beauty, although all of them were sophisticated, beautiful in their own way. The gowns they wore were expensive, their jewelry a fashion show in itself.

Bolt could read Tom's mind as each of the girls was presented, and he knew that it was all Tom could do not to comment on their various qualities. Annabelle Snyder, daughter of Joseph and Catherine Snyder, was by far the most buxom of the debutantes. She was also the most flirtatious as she walked along the red carpeted path. She was a blue-eyed blonde who exuded sex as she moved across the floor, coyly batting her eyelashes at the young men who were attending the Ball, wriggling her hips as she walked. Her flame-red gown clung to her curves. The scooped neckline was low enough so the tops of her creamy white breasts were exposed.

As Annabelle took her place between her parents, Bolt caught Tom's eye. Tom grinned, rolled his eyes upward and took a deep breath. Bolt knew exactly what he was thinking. Probably the same thing as every other man and boy in the room.

After the last debutante was presented, the orchestra played a waltz and, by tradition, the fathers of the girls danced the first dance with their lovely daughters.

Even before the waltz was over, Emory Howes had joined Bolt and Tom and was pestering them to go with him so he could show them the big surprise he had planned for them. Bolt wanted to wait until he had a chance to talk to Valerie. He didn't know whether it was proper to congratulate her on the event of her debut, but at least he wanted to speak to her, compliment her on how lovely she looked.

Bolt kept his eyes on the dance floor and when the first dance ended, he thought Rodney Blair would bring Valerie back over. Instead, Valerie was approached by a young man who began dancing with her when the music began again. Annabelle Snyder danced by Bolt a few times, in the arms of another man, and she always made a point to smile at Bolt, bat her eyelashes at him.

After two more dances and watching Valerie dance with different men, it was evident to Bolt that she would be tied up until the members of the orchestra decided to take an intermission. He finally agreed to accompany Howes, providing they would not be gone very long.

"You'll forget all about Valerie when you see what I've got in store for you," Emory insisted.

"Valerie is the only reason I'm here," Bolt explained. "But let's go see your big surprise while she's busy so I can get back. Come on, Tom, you're in on this too."

"Time for me to get another drink. You go on

without me."

"Not this time, my friend. I'm sure Mister Howes wants to honor you, too. Besides, you haven't had the pleasure of Howes' company yet." Bolt was sure that Emory didn't understand the sarcasm in the words, but Tom knew.

"Of course," said Emory. "This is for both of you."

"But I'd rather stay here and watch the girls."

"Come on, Tom. You're not getting out of it this time."

Emory led the two men through a side door that went from the ballroom to a smaller room, then down a long hall that led to a back door. As they walked along the hall toward the back of the building, Bolt got a whiff of food cooking. He thought about Bing Chee and wondered if he was having a good time.

Outside, Emory led them down a dimly-lit path, toward the bungalows that spilled filtered light from their curtained windows. A single lantern hung above the door of each separate cottage. Emory opened the unlocked door of the middle bungalow, invited Bolt and Tom inside.

Bolt was prepared for the sight he saw when he stepped inside. His breath caught in his throat for an instant before he was able to regain his composure. Inside the small cottage were ten of the most beautiful prostitutes he'd ever seen gathered in one place, all of them dressed in extremely brief costumes. That was shock enough but the thing that really stunned him was the fact that the girls were not all of the same race or color. In fact, there were two girls of each. White, Indian, Chinese, Black and Mexican. He wondered how such a variety of girls had been collected. He knew there were many Chinese people in the Barbary Coast area, but they were too far north to see any Mexican families or Black families and he hadn't seen an Indian in many a moon.

"These girls are here for your pleasure," Emory announced proudly. "Take your choice."

"You're kidding," Tom grinned as he looked each girl over.

"No, I'm not kidding," said Emory. "When the Shorecliff Club puts on a party, it goes all the way. These lovely ladies have been provided for any of the gentlemen guests who wish to partake, but I wanted you to have first crack at them."

"Jeez," said Tom, "you mean the fellows come out here screw around with their wives so close? That could be risky."

"Not at all," Emory said. "It's not unusual for gentlemen to step outside to smoke a cigar during the Ball. The wives never know the difference. It's all handled very discreetly. If it weren't for diversions like this, some of these men wouldn't even attend these formal affairs. So, you see, it benefits the wives."

Bolt narrowed his eyes to slits as he looked at Emory Howes.

"Does Rodney Blair know about this? About the girls being out here?"

"No, uh, I'm afraid he wouldn't understand," Emory stammered. "He's rather stuffy about such things. But I can tell you're a real man and you know there's nothing wrong with taking a little pleasure when it's offered."

"Who provided the girls, Howes? You?"

"Well, uh, you might say I had a hand in it. But I'm not the only one."

"What you're saying is that you're running a private little bordello out here. That must bring in a nice little profit."

"Oh, no, you've got it all wrong. The guests aren't charged for these services. The girls are provided strictly for entertainment and pleasure."

"Someone's paying for it," Bolt said, his voice almost accusing. "Girls like this don't come cheap. Who pays for them? The Club?"

"I'm afraid the financial arrangements are confidential. You'd have to ask someone else."

Bolt saw Emory pull his stiff shirt collar away from his neck, a gesture that signalled he was becoming uneasy under the questioning. Bolt realized he was being rude to Howes for asking questions that were really none of his business. After all, Howes was trying to please them to show his gratitude for them saving Valerie's life.

Bolt dropped the subject and looked at the girls who were smiling with sensual lips. They were sending sexual signals with their scantily clad bodies, enticing Bolt and Tom with their charms. The girls began to move toward them and before Bolt knew what was happening, he was surrounded by a bevy of beautiful women. Tom was getting the same attention as the girls peppered them with kisses. The girls ran their hands through Bolt's hair, across his body, fondled the bulge between his legs.

That's when Bolt noticed something that rang a bell of recognition deep in his mind. That's when he

84

thought of Penny and her black eye. One of the girls who was fondling Bolt had a dark bruise on her upper arm. Bolt looked more carefully at the other girls then. He saw that two of the other girls were bruised, one of them with a cut across her cheek, the other with bruises on both her arms and legs. He thought about Penny's story about being kidnapped and wondered if there was any connection with these girls. There was only one way he could find out.

"Thank you," he said to Howes. "It was very thoughtful of you to bring us out here. Think we'll stay and take advantage of your offer."

Emory smiled, pleased with himself. "Good. There are separate cottages for your privacy. Use any one of them. They all have porch lanterns. Just carry the lantern inside when you go there and you will not be disturbed. Choose any girl you wish."

"Can I take two girls?" Tom grinned.

"Take as many as you wish," Emory said. Satisfied that he had pleased the two heroes, he wished them a good time, then left them to their own pleasures as he headed back to the main building before he was missed.

The cottage on the far end of the line of small buildings was the only one that did not have a burning porch lantern hanging outside. An orange glow filtered through the heavy curtains draped across the window of one of the two rooms of the cottage. The window of the other room was dark.

Inside, Jubal Naylor stood in the dark room, peeking through the curtain he had pulled aside. He knew he could not be seen from the outside.

A few minutes earlier, he had seen Emory Howes walk along the path to the middle bungalow with two party guests in tow. Jubal hadn't recognized either of the men, but it didn't matter to him. He and the Chinaman were being paid an enormous sum, over two thousand dollars, just to provide the girls for the party. He wondered who was footing the bill for the services of the girls, but there were some things the Chinaman didn't tell him. He didn't really care as long as he got his cut of the action.

It was Jubal's job to deliver the girls to the party and see that the girls were returned safely to the whorehouse. He liked that part of the job because he figured there would be a little extra money in it for him. In most private parties of this type where the guests were not expected to pay for the services of the prostitutes, it was a common practice for the men to leave a generous tip for the girls. Before he took the girls back to the bordello, Jubal would shake them down. Any money they had collected during the evening would be confiscated and pocketed by him. It would be little enough compensation for spending the entire evening in the tiny cottage, waiting until it was time to take the girls back.

Of course, he had brought along his favorite prostitute, Jewel. She was by far the sexiest girl in the group and he had banged her more than once. Their names were similar, but they had other things in common, too. For one thing, they were both devious. Jewel had tried several sneaky tricks to try to escape from the bordello, but each time, Jubal had outsmarted her, stopping her just before she got away. She had been punished severely the first time she had tried to escape and she still bore the bruises from that episode. But he didn't bother with the punishment anymore. It had become more of a game between the two of them and Jubal always won.

Before the evening was over, Jubal would bring Jewel to his cottage and have his way with her, but right now he was pouting. He resented the fact that his Chinese boss, Woo Fong, was attending the party as a respected guest while he himself was considered a member of the lower class of society and would not dare show his face at the social gathering.

There was another aspect of the party that was getting under Jubal's skin. From the cottage, he could see the glimmering lights of the mansion, could hear the laughter, the strains of the orchestra. He knew that even the servants were being treated better than he was tonight. But the thing that bothered him most was that he knew Valerie Blair was one of the debutantes. He could imagine her pretty face, her shapely body.

To Jubal, Valerie Blair was the cream of the crop, so to speak. Not only was she sexy, but except for Woo Fong, her father was the wealthiest man in San Francisco. She was also the most unobtainable. Maybe that's why he wanted her so much. He wanted to put the boots to her time after time and when he tired of her, he would rent her out for top prices, maybe even five hundred dollars a shot. And all of the money would be his. Woo Fong would know nothing of this. After a couple of weeks, he would demand ransom money from her father. His plan would work. He was too smart to get caught.

Kidnapping Valerie Blair had become an obsession

with Jubal. At times, like now, it was all he thought about. If he could pull it off tonight, in the middle of her coming-out party, it would be the most brilliant coup of the century.

The sound of someone walking outside brought him back to reality. He peeked out the darkened window again, saw Emory Howes returning to the mansion.

A thought struck Jubal. If he could get inside the mansion without being noticed, he could carry out his plan to kidnap Valerie. He couldn't let Howes know what he was up to because Howes would be the first one to ruin him if he knew about the Blair girl. But Howes could be helpful, just the same.

Emory Howes could be the key to getting into the party where, at this very minute, Valerie Blair would be the Belle of the Ball.

Chapter Nine

Bolt chose the girl with the ugly bruise on her upper arm. Not for sexual favors, but he wanted to get her alone, ask her some questions, see if she knew anything about Penny.

He took her by the arm, led her to the bungalow next to the middle one, leaving Tom to pick between the other nine girls. If he knew Tom, his best friend wasn't kidding about taking two of the girls to another bungalow.

As per Howes' instructions, Bolt reached up and took the burning porch lantern from its hook, carried it inside, an indication to others that the cottage was occupied. The small, individual building, like the others in the row, had two rooms. Bolt checked the sitting room and the bedroom to be sure they were alone before he set the lantern on a table in the sitting room. The furnishings in the cottage were plush and expensive, as he had expected. A closet in the bedroom contained nightgowns of varying degrees of briefness and colors. A choice for any man's tastes and fantasies.

"Sit down," Bolt said, motioning to the long divan near the low table where the lantern was.

The girl was surprised that he did not take her directly into the bedroom, but she did as she was ordered. Bolt sat down at the other end of the couch, facing her.

"What's your name?" he asked.

"Jewel."

"Just Jewel? No last name?"

"Just Jewel."

That was the same response he had gotten from Penny the night before. No last name. Just a first name that rang phony in his mind. It was as if the girls had been taught what to say and what not to say.

"My name's Bolt," he began.

"Just Bolt?" she smiled. "No last name?"

"Bolt is my last name," he laughed, "but it's the only name I use." The two of them had established an instant rapport and he saw Jewel begin to relax.

"I like the name," she said.

"How'd you get that bruise on your arm?" Bolt asked abruptly. He watched her reaction. She squinted her eyes, tensed briefly, then settled back in the soft couch.

"Just ran into a door," she said casually.

"I thought that was the excuse reserved for black eyes," he said, his eyes locked into hers. "What about those other girls over there? Did they get their bruises by running into a door, too? The one with the cut cheek? The one with black and blue marks all over her arms and legs? Looks like you got off easy with just one bruise."

"I can't speak for the other girls," she said. "I barely know them. In fact I never saw them before tonight."

"Oh? You work at the same whorehouse, don't you?"

"Yes, but ..."

"But you never see anyone else because you're locked in your room, away from all other contacts except for the johns you service."

"I ... I ..."

"That's what I learned from a girl I met last night. A girl named Penny." Again, Bolt watched for some reaction. The girl did not show any signs of recognizing the name. "She had just escaped from a customer's home, but she did it because she was being held prisoner at a whorehouse."

"Really? She got away with it?" Jewel's face brightened.

"I don't know. I left her alone for a few minutes in a hotel room where I was hiding her and when I got back, she was gone." He saw Jewel's eyes darken again. She changed positions, looked perfectly composed again.

"Sorry to hear about your friend," she said.

"Any chance she worked at the same whorehouse where you work?"

"Where did she work?"

"That's just it. She never knew the name of the whorehouse. She was blindfolded when she was delivered to the whorehouse. Said she had been seasick for days from the boat ride."

The shiver that coursed through Jewel's body was almost undetectable, but Bolt saw it and wondered if she was remembering something from her past or just reacting to another girl's troubles.

"Sad what some people will go through just to get to San Francisco," Jewel said with no feeling.

"She didn't come here by choice. Where do you work?"

"At the House of Paradise. It's the finest bordello in the area."

"With the highest prices, I'm told."

"The girls are all high-classed. The men get their money's worth."

"I'm sure they do. Think Penny worked there?"

"I really can't say. Did you come here to talk or to be pleasured? There will be other men along shortly and I must get back soon."

"Shouldn't matter to you what we do together. You're not getting your share of the profits. You don't get any money at all. You're nothing more than a sex slave."

Bolt saw the anger flare up in her eyes, the sudden flush to her cheeks. Good. He wanted her mad. Mad enough to give him some answers.

"I'm not a slave," she snapped. "I get a clean room, good food and ..."

"And no money! That makes you a slave! Tell me, Jewel, did you choose this kind of a life for yourself or were you forced into it and then decided you liked it so much you never wanted to get away?"

The tears came then. Jewel lowered her head, dabbed at the corners of her eyes. She had become so hardened in the past two weeks, she had forgotten that she had feelings of her own.

Bolt moved closer to her, put his arm around her

shoulder.

"It's okay, Jewel. I'm a friend. Maybe I can help you. You were kidnapped, too, weren't you?"

"Yes," she said softly. "It's been so bad you can't imagine."

"Penny said she was threatened with her life if she tried to escape or if she told anyone about her plight."

"She worked at the House of Paradise, I'm sure, even though I never knew her. I was kidnapped, too, brought here by Santa Rosa up north. My father owns a winery up there. My family is very wealthy. It would kill them if they ever found out that I was a prostitute now. I fought it at first, but I finally gave up because I knew how much it would hurt them if they found out."

"Maybe it's hurting them even more not knowing where you are. If you can give me the information I need I will try my best to set you free. The other girls, too. How many girls are there?"

"I don't know. Maybe twenty at a time. But they are always different faces. Sometimes we're allowed to eat our meals together, but we're well guarded and not allowed to talk to each other. But I've seen their faces. Always changing. Some leave, new ones come."

"Where do the girls go when they leave the bordello?"

"I don't know. From what I've heard, some of them are sent to private homes or ranches to work as slaves. As far as I know, none of them has ever escaped. At least that's what Jubal told me."

"Jubal? That's the name Penny mentioned."

"Yes. Jubal Naylor. He owns the bordello. He's

taken a special liking to me. He sends for me whenever the mood strikes him. I guess I'm luckier than most of the girls. At least I haven't been beaten since that first time when I tried to escape."

"How does Naylor kidnap all of the girls? He must be working with someone."

"Jubal's bordello is only a front for the kidnap ring, a place to keep the girls for a while and still make a profit from them. The head man is a Chinaman. I've heard Jubal bitch about him often enough."

"You know his name?"

"No. Jubal just calls him 'the Chinaman' but never mentions his name."

"Do you think you can find out his name?"

"Maybe. Jubal likes me enough that he just might let it slip if I can steer the conversation in the right direction."

"I need to know when the next boat load of girls is due to dock. Might be able to catch whoever's bringing them in. Might even catch the Chinaman with the goods."

"I think I can find out, but I don't think all the girls arrive by boat. I heard one girl complain about having splinters in her arms and legs from riding in a coach all the way from Texas. She was taken out of the dining area right after she said it and I never did see her again."

"See what you can find out."

"But how will I get the message to you? I'm not allowed to leave the bordello."

"I'll visit you there. Think you can find out by tomorrow night?"

"Yes, but you'll have to pay before they'll let you see me."

"Don't worry about that. We'd better be going."

"But aren't you going to make love to me?" she pouted.

"Tomorrow night," he smiled. "If I'm going to pay a hundred bucks to see you, I'm sure as hell going to get my money's worth."

Jewel laughed for the first time in weeks.

"Go on back to your party," she said. "I'm supposed to stay in here long enough to wash up, freshen up for the next customer before I go back to the other cottage. I'll hang the lantern back outside when I leave."

She got up when Bolt did, reached over and hugged him. When he kissed her on the mouth, her lips were soft and warm, only a promise of things to come when he saw her again.

On the way back to the main building, something startled Bolt. A noise. A rustle of the bushes near the path. He paused, listened, heard it again. He wished he had worn his pistol, but he had thought it would not be proper to wear it with the formal attire. He also thought there would be no need for it, but now he felt naked without it. Perhaps a squirrel had run across the path, or maybe he had startled a sleeping bird with his footsteps.

He walked on, slowly, saw the shadowy figure in the bushes just before he got there. With lightning speed, he leaped at the figure, grabbed the man by the collar and jerked him out on the path where he could see him.

It was Merle Stamps, the reporter for the San

Francisco Chronicle, who was just as startled as Bolt was.

"What in the hell are you doing here?" Bolt barked. "You some kind of pervert? A peeping Tom?"

"I was just trying to get a story," he said, shaking in his boots.

"About what? The birds and the bees?"

"No, sir. Just getting some background material for the story about the party."

"Then I suggest you come back to the party with me. You can get all the material you need there."

The two men walked to the back door of the mansion together. Just before they went inside, the reporter spoke again.

"I'm really working on a bigger story than the party," Stamps said. "Do you think someone was trying to kidnap Valerie Blair during the fire?"

His question caught Bolt off guard. "Why do you ask that?"

"Someone told me they saw Gimpy coming out the back door of the yardage shop just after the fire started. Gimpy wouldn't be in there buying fabric, that's for sure. I'm investigating rumors about a kidnap ring that's operating in the area and I thought maybe Gimpy was working for someone who wanted to kidnap Valerie."

"What do you know about the kidnappings?" Bolt asked.

"I can't tell you anything I know until the story breaks. I just wondered about Valerie. I know you were there."

"Well, I'm staying at the Pelican Point Hotel if

you ever want to talk about it. I just may be able to help you."

One of the guests came out the door just then. Bolt and Stamps let him by, then went on inside. The subject was dropped with no further discussion. Bolt knew that Stamps wasn't about to reveal any of his information and Bolt wouldn't volunteer what he knew until after he had talked to Jewel again.

When Bolt entered the ballroom, the orchestra was getting ready to play again. Before he could walk more than five steps into the room, Annabelle Snyder came up to him, brushed the blonde hair back from her face.

"Hi," she said. "I've been looking all over for you and your friend. I just wanted to shake your hand. I've never met a real hero before." She took Bolt's hand, then stood on tiptoes, stretched to kiss Bolt on the cheek.

Bolt felt the warmth of her body as she pressed her breasts against him. Embarrassed, he glanced around to see if anyone was watching.

"This is your big night, isn't it?" Bolt said, treating her like a little girl. "I'll bet you're excited."

"Oh, yes! It's a night I'll never forget. I actually got to kiss you! I think I'm going to swoon."

"Well, don't do it here, Miss Snyder. I'm not much of a hand at catching girls."

"Will you dance the next dance with me?" she said, batting her large blue eyes.

"Well, actually, right now I'm looking for Valerie. I'm her guest and I haven't even talked to her yet." Bolt looked around the room, spotted Valerie across the room. She was looking right at him. "There she is now."

"Maybe another dance later, then," Annabelle pouted, then bounced away to flirt with another young man.

"Well, finally," Bolt said when he walked up to Valerie. "The evening's half gone and I'm just getting a chance to talk to you. You look lovely tonight, Valerie."

"Thank you. I saw you leave with Mister Howes. I was hoping he wouldn't keep you hopping all night. I figured he took you back to the kitchen to sample the midnight supper. But I'm glad you're back."

"Me, too." Bolt found himself suddenly speechless. Valerie was so beautiful, so close. It was all he could do to keep from taking her in his arms and kissing her in front of all the people.

"The next dance belongs to us," she said softly.

"I hope so. You're so popular I couldn't get near you before."

"You didn't try very hard."

"To tell you the truth, I'm not much of a dancer. You take your life in your hands, or toes, when you dance with me."

"I'll risk it," she breathed as another waltz began.

Neither of them talked as they floated across the dance floor. Bolt was lighter on his feet than he thought he would be and he attributed it to the fact that he was with Valerie and some things just came naturally when you were with a beautiful young girl. He knew that as the dance progressed, they were dancing too close to each other. He could feel her warmth through the layers of cloth between them. He felt the tug at his manhood, felt it begin to swell. He hoped it would go away before the end of the dance so no one would notice.

When the dance ended, Valerie looked up at Bolt, a dreamy look in her eyes.

"Bolt, I'm not feeling well. I think I need a little air."

"It is close in here. I'll take you out on the veranda for awhile."

"I'd rather go for a buggy ride. Get away from the noise for a time."

"Think your folks would mind?"

"No. I'll tell them we're going. Wait for me out in the lobby."

Bolt waited for her and a few minutes later, she appeared with a smile on her face, a white lace shawl draped across her shoulders, covering the top of her velvet gown.

"What did they say?" he asked.

"They said if I was feeling faint, a buggy ride would be good for me. They don't want me sick on my big night. They said it would be fine as long as I took Bing Chee along."

"You want me to get him?"

"No. I wouldn't think of bothering him tonight, I know he's having a good time and I can't see spoiling it. I can trust you to be a gentleman, can't I?"

Bolt saw the twinkle in her eye.

"You can trust me, but I'm not so sure I can trust you," he laughed.

"Maybe you can't," she teased.

Chapter Ten

Valerie didn't have to worry about getting her pale blue dress dirty. The buggy had been scrubbed down from top to bottom, the brass fixtures hand-polished to a high gleam. After Bing Chee had parked the buggy with the others in the cleared field, he had meticulously wiped the leather seats off in case road dust had clung to the upholstery. He would go over the carriage again just before the time the guests were to depart from the ball.

Bing Chee took great pride in his work as a servant for the Blairs. He was well paid by Rodney Blair, but it was not the money that made him a happy man. The Blairs treated him and the other servants like family. They treated him with respect and he did everything he could to deserve that respect.

Bolt helped Valerie up into the carriage, then went around and got up in the seat beside her. He took the reins in hand, turned the carriage around and headed down the lamp-lit road that led away from the Shore-cliff Club. He glanced over at Valerie and smiled. She looked radiant in the lamp glow, her blue eyes sparkling, a natural flush to her cheeks.

"Sorry you're not feeling well," Bolt said. "Too much excitement on your big night?"

"I feel perfectly well," she announced as she fluffed the folds of her full skirt around her legs. She cocked her head, tossed her dark curls back with the flip of her hand. Her blue eyes drove into Bolt's eyes. "I just wanted to get away from there for awhile. Be alone with you. This was the only way I knew how to do it without having a proper chaperone along."

Bolt felt the flutter in his stomach as he looked at her, the jab of desire at his loins. He knew what she wanted. He could read it in her eyes. He just didn't know if she knew what she wanted. She was like a small bird testing her wings for the first time. He saw the look of hunger in her eyes, the need to express her growing sexuality. The Debutante Ball was more than a ritual of presenting eighteen-year-old girls to society. It was an announcement that they were young women, fully developed and capable of taking the responsibilities of womanhood. Valerie was ripe and fair pickings.

"Can't say as I blame you," Bolt said. "Kinda makes your head spin after awhile, being in that room with all those people."

"That isn't what I meant," she pouted, turning her head to look straight ahead. "I just wanted to be alone with you."

"Well, here I am," he grinned. "Do with me what you would."

"I just might," she said, her voice showing a spark of determination.

"Where would you like to go?"

"To your place." She looked over at him again.

Bolt heard the challenge in her voice. He melted under her bold stare.

"It's your night, Princess."

Bolt followed the road down the hill, up another hill and down to the Pelican Point Hotel, which was not too far from the Shorecliff Club but could not be seen there because of the rolling terrain. He drove the carriage around to the back of the hotel, got down and tied the horse to a hitching post. He walked around to Valerie's side where she was sitting prim and proper in the seat, the full skirt of her blue ball gown fluffed around her.

Bolt raised his hands to help her down from the carriage. She stuck out a blue satin slipper, stepped down onto the metal step, then lowered her arms to accept Bolt's help. As she slid down into his arms, he felt her body press against him. He steadied her and when she regained her balance, she lingered in his arms, her red moist lips only an inch away from his. He was drawn to her like a magnet as he felt the heat radiate from her body, as he smelled her sweet scent. For a brief instant, he thought she was going to kiss him. His lips parted in anticipation as desire tugged at his manhood. But their lips didn't come together. Instead, Valerie turned her head away, took a step backwards and looped her arm through his.

"Can you see the ocean from your room?" Valerie asked.

"During the day. At night there isn't much to see except the waves splashing on to the shore."

"Sounds romantic. I still haven't thanked you

properly for saving my life yesterday, you know." She looked up at him and smiled, squeezed his hand.

"No need to, ma'am."

"For me there is. I was brought up to pay my dues and I owe you a debt."

Bolt took her in the back door of the Pelican Point Hotel. They went up the back stairs to the second floor instead of walking around through the lobby. In the light from the lanterns in the hall, Bolt unlocked his door, opened it wide. After Valerie went inside, he reached for the matches to light the lamp on the table next to the door. Before he could pick up the matches, he felt her hand on his.

"Don't light the lantern just yet. I want to see the ocean." She strolled over to the window and peered through it. Until Bolt closed the door to his room, she saw only the reflection of the hall light in the door frame.

After Bolt closed and locked the door, he walked across the darkened room, joined Valerie at the window. He opened the window, breathed in the crisp ocean air. The fragrance of Valerie's perfume floated on the evening breeze, made Bolt aware of her femininity. He glanced over at her, saw the shine to her dark hair, the profile of her lovely face with its small delicate nose, the soft full lips.

"I was right. It is romantic," she said as she stared down at the glimmering ocean waves. "Even the moonlight makes it a perfect night. The moon's full, isn't it?"

"Almost. It's still missing a chunk at the bottom." Bolt leaned closer to the open window, pointed up at the moon.

Valerie reached up and took his hand. She brought it down to her face, rubbed it along her smooth cheek. She turned to face him, her eyes burning into his.

Bolt held her gaze for a long moment. He felt a surge of heat between his legs as his manhood began to swell. He took her in his arms, pulled her close to him and kissed her hard on the mouth. Her lips parted as he slid his tongue deep into the warmth of her mouth. He felt her body melt into his as she drew herself up close to him. Even through the thickness of the folds of her skirt, he could feel the pressure of her body against his loins. He tasted the sweetness of her mouth, smelled the flowery scent of her perfume, the fresh aroma of soap in her hair. Her lithe body was soft and pliable in his arms and he wanted to hold her for a long time. His kiss was hard and passionate and she responded with a passion of her own, flicking her tongue against his.

"I want you, Bolt," she husked when they came up for air.

"You sure, Valerie?"

"Yes," she said, her breath warm on his ear. "It's my way of thanking you for saving my life. I want you to take my virginity. It's the only thing I have to offer you."

"You're not obligated to me. If that's the only reason ..."

"It's not the only reason," she said, cutting off his words. "Ever since I first saw you, when I opened my eyes after you carried me outside of the burning building, I knew I wanted you. You're so ... so much a man. The way you look at me with those bold blue eyes. And when you smile at me, your lips are so sensual, I can hardly stand it. The few men who have come courting me have been so stuffy, so proper. Like they're trying to impress my father instead of me. But you're different. You're so sure of yourself. And in case nobody ever told you, you're very sexy."

She threw her arms around him and kissed him again. This time, she put her whole body into it, pushing into his crotch with her loins, rubbing her pliant breasts against his chest. She burned his lips with the heat of her kiss, the pressure of her passion.

"What about your pretty evening gown? And your fancy hairdo?"

"I was under the impression people took their clothes off when they did it and I don't care about my hair," she said, her voice indignant with frustration. "I don't understand you. I thought men wanted it all the time. But I don't think you want me at all."

"Yes, I do," Bolt said, taking her in his arms again.

She stepped back away from him, turned and walked across the room.

"Then why all the excuses? I'll bet if it was Annabelle Snyder, you wouldn't hesitate."

"What's that supposed to mean?"

"I saw the way Annabelle was making eyes at you. She's got quite a reputation. Sleeps with every man she can get her hands on. If I were you . . ." Valerie caught herself in the middle of the sentence. "Forgive me. That wasn't a nice thing to say."

"If it's true, nothing wrong with saying it."

"It's true, but it's not my place to talk about her. I guess with the excitement of the Debutante Ball, I'm not myself tonight.''

''I thought you society gals were accustomed to these fancy parties.''

''I am not a society gal!'' she snapped. ''My father happens to be wealthy, but I'm a human being with real feelings and emotions. I'm tired of being thought of as the rich daughter of Rodney Blair. I thought you were different! I had planned to save myself for the man I married, but when you came into my life, I knew I wanted you. I wanted you to be the first. Does that make me such a bad person?''

Bolt grabbed her and held her tight in his arms. After a minute, he kissed her, more tenderly than before. He felt her soften in his arms, felt her respond to his kiss with warm lips. Her body trembled against him.

''You cold?'' he asked.

''No. I'm . . . I feel all funny and tingly inside.''

''Does this damn dress come off?'' he said, fumbling at the smooth slippery buttons at the back of her dress.

She moved back, quickly slipped the satin buttons out of their loops. She pushed the bodice and sleeves down over her arms, stepped out of the full skirt. The dress crumpled to the floor with a soft rustling sound. She picked it up, carefully draped it over a chair near the window.

As she was taking care of her dress, Bolt quickly undressed, let his clothes fall to the floor in a heap. He walked over to the window and stood beside her as she removed the two full petticoats she wore beneath the dress. He reached up and undid the buttons on the front of her lace camisole, slid the thin straps over the smooth skin of her shoulders. Her full breasts were like polished copper in the moonlight. He cupped his hands under them, lowered his head to kiss each one of them in turn. His hands moved across her smooth flesh, down her sides where his fingers tucked inside the band of her panties. He pushed the panties down her hips, let them fall to her ankles. He looked down and saw the dark furry mound nestled in among the golden moonlit skin. When he touched her between her legs, she gasped. he slid a finger across the crease of her sex, found that she was already damp.

His swollen manhood throbbed when he felt the heat of her sex. He swirled his finger around the burning flesh of her pussy lips, eased the finger into the honey-oiled slit.

"Oh, ohhhhh," she sighed. "That feels sooooo good. I'm tingling all over."

Bolt scooped her up in his arms, carried her over to the bed and dropped her down gently. He crawled in next to her warm, pliant body, propped himself up on one arm and kissed her with a hard passion, his tongue sliding in and out of her mouth. He threw his leg over one of her legs, reached for her breast at the same time. He lowered his head, kissed the breast, then took the nipple into his mouth, suckled it.

"Touch me down there again," she begged.

"You touch me, too," he said. He took her hand, placed it on his hardened shaft. She started to draw her hand away, but then wrapped her fingers around it. The warmth of her hand on his sensitive skin sent a shoot of desire through his loins. His cock twitched in her hand. She tightened her grip around him, then moved her hand up and down the length of his throbbing cock.

"You're so big," she gasped. "Will you ... will you fit?"

"Yes. If you relax when it's time." He reached down, spread her legs slightly and placed his hand on her furry mound. He ran his fingers around her sensitive flesh, slipped his finger inside her damp portal.

"Mmmmmmm. You don't know what you're doing to me," she sighed.

"You still want me?" He didn't really care what her answer was. He had no intention of stopping now.

"Yes. I'm so hot I can hardly stand it."

"Then it's time." He moved over her body, straddled her legs, positioned himself above her. He looked down at the smooth flesh of her body that was stippled by a shaft of moonlight. She was like an ancient goddess waiting for a ceremonial sacrifice to happen, her nude body sheathed in gold. He was ready to sink into her buried treasure and take whatever she offered.

His swollen shaft hung in the air, poised and aimed like an arrow at her pussy. He reached down and spread her legs wide apart. Once again, he fingered her entrance, splayed the lips open so he could enter her. He dipped his rigid shaft down until it touched her glistening warm pussylips. He gave a gentle thrust, pushed in until he bumped against the barrier of her maidenhead. He felt her legs stiffen, her body tense beneath him.

"Relax," he whispered in her ear. He backed out of her steaming portal, then plunged in with his driving rod. He felt the membrane give way to his thrust. He sank deep inside her, where it was wet and warm. As he slid easily in and out of her, he felt her body relax and respond to his deep strokes. Her muscles were like a tight fist around his shaft, keeping him deep inside her steaming cauldron.

He was surprised by her eagerness, her passion, as she bucked and squirmed on the bed beneath him. She groaned, threw her legs up in the air, wrapped them around Bolt's back. The sound of the ocean waves crashing at the shoreline were now muffled by the heavy breathing in the room, the creaking bed, the slapping sound of the naked bodies coming together. Bolt was mindless to the sounds around him, though. The exhilarating sexual sensation that pulsed through him wiped out any other thought. He pounded into her with long deep strokes, unable to hold back when he felt his seed begin to boil.

He grabbed her tightly, crushed her lips with a hard passionate kiss. He plunged in deep one more time, shoving his shaft to the hilt, holding it there as his seed spilled over and splashed against the folds of her silky cavern. He moaned with the ultimate pleasure, but he could not talk for an instant. He could not even think. It was several minutes before he could find the strength to roll off of her sweat-covered body and collapse beside her.

"Bolt?" she said, after a few minutes.

"Yeah?"

"Was it good for you?"

"Magnificent! You're a little tiger. You surprised me."

"I surprised myself. I can't even describe how good it felt to have you inside me. I . . . I want you again."

"I want you, too, but it will have to wait until another time. We've got to get back to the Ball before your father discovers we didn't take Bing Chee along as a chaperone. Wouldn't want him to send a posse out looking for me for kidnapping his daughter for immoral purposes."

"What we did wasn't immoral, was it, Bolt? I mean, some folks would say so, wouldn't they?"

"People tend to have their own opinions of what's right and wrong, but you have to do what feels right to you. What we did was right for us. We both wanted it and we're both adults." He hopped out of bed, slapped her on her bare buttocks. "Now get dressed so we can get back."

As he lit the lantern, Valerie slid to the edge of the bed, then stood up. Bolt wanted her again when he saw her lovely curvaceous body, her firm breasts and flaring hips. Instead, he put the black tuxedo and tie back on, the white shirt with its stiff collar, the black shoes and socks. It still felt odd not to be wearing his gunbelt and holstered pistol.

"Do you think anyone will know?" Valerie asked as she stood in front of the mirror and brushed her damp, straggly curls back into place. Her blue dress was unwrinkled and looked just as nice as it had before.

"They'll know," Bolt grinned. "There's no hiding that rosy glow in your cheeks."

Chapter Eleven

Jubal Naylor was able to get the uniform of a Shorecliff Club servant with very little trouble. He had called out to Emory Howes as he left the bungalow where the prostitutes waited, had asked him if he could find an extra uniform for him. Anxious to please, Howes had told Naylor that the extra uniforms were kept in a closet in one of the upstairs bedrooms where the Club employees changed clothes before reporting for work. Howes hadn't asked any questions. He just delivered the fresh uniform fifteen minutes later.

After he had changed clothes, placing the cap on his head so that the bill would hide his face, he went searching for Valerie Blair. He knew that he would not be easily recognized as long as he didn't run into the Chinaman, Woo Fong.

He entered the back door of the main building, keeping his head low. When he finally entered the main ballroom, he stayed near the wall, glanced around, but didn't see Valerie. He moved to his left, keeping a careful watch out for Woo Fong so that he wouldn't accidentally bump into him. He spotted a dark-haired girl at the table that was being used for a bar, watched her until he could see her face. Finally the girl, who was with other people, turned enough so that he could see her profile. Jubal was standing quite a distance away but he was certain the girl was Valerie. No two girls could be that beautiful.

Just to make sure, he strolled to the bar, stood at one end so that he could get a good look at her face. He kept his head down as if looking at the bottles in front of him. Out of the corner of his eye, he sensed that her head was finally turned in his direction. He looked up quickly, was shocked when he realized that it was not Valerie but someone who looked enough like her to be her twin sister. Or maybe an older sister. He saw the woman reach out and take a cup of punch from the uniformed man who was tending bar. She thanked him, turned back to the man beside her.

"You're welcome, Missus Blair," the bartender said.

Naylor looked at her again. She looked too young to be Valerie's mother, but that must be who she was.

"You want a drink, Joe?"

Jubal looked up when he realized the bartender was talking to him. He glanced down at the bottles in front of him.

"Whiskey," he said.

"How's it going?" the bartender said when he handed Jubal the drink.

"Good," was his short reply.

"I figured you'd be getting cold out there opening the door for all these people."

So the bartender had mistaken him for the doorman. There was a resemblance at that. Jubal had noticed the doorman when he had ridden by the front door earlier when he delivered the girls to the back cottages. Jubal knew that extra help had been hired for the large party and evidently the bartender didn't know the other servants too well. Could be that the doorman was new too.

"That Missus Blair sure is a purty woman," said the bartender. "Looks young enough to be Valerie's sister, wouldn't you say?"

"Yep." Jubal turned and scanned the crowd again. "Where is Valerie?"

"Guess you weren't here when her mother said she wasn't feeling well and had gone for a ride with Mister Bolt. About a half an hour ago. Didn't you see them leave?"

"That must have been when I left to take a leak," Jubal lied. There was that name again. Bolt. It kept cropping up at the wrong times. That man seemed to be everywhere. He was like a dark shadow, haunting him, striking always just before Jubal got there.

"You're lucky you've got someone to spell you. I've been here for almost two hours waiting for someone to relieve me."

The bartender's remarks gave Jubal an idea. If Valerie and that Bolt fellow were still gone, it stood to reason that sooner or later they would have to come in the front door. Maybe he'd just go spell the real doorman. He'd be waiting for them when they returned. It would be easier that way. There were never any people around the front door while the party was going on.

113

"Cheers," said Jubal. He nodded to the bartender and moved away, relieved that it had been so easy to move about the room without being noticed.

Bolt eased the Blair buggy into the same spot where Bing Chee had stored it earlier. He walked around the front of the buggy, helped Valerie down, making sure that her long gown didn't hit the dusty ground.

Before they headed back to the party, she tipped her face up and kissed him again. She was glad that he was the first. He was very special to her. They took their time strolling back to the mansion, walking hand in hand.

At the bottom of the steps, she kissed him again. She knew the doorman was watching them, but she didn't care. Nobody else was around and doormen were supposed to be discreet about what they saw.

The doorman watched them climb up the stairs, nodded to them when they reached the top of the steps. He purposely stood at the edge of the porch, several feet away from the door.

"Nice evening for a buggy ride," Jubal Naylor said, studying Bolt's face.

"Yes, it is," Bolt answered him. "A bit chilly, but nice."

"You're Mister Bolt, aren't you?" Jubal asked.

"Yes."

"There was someone looking for you a while ago. Said your friend, Mister Penrod, had been hurt. Said if you showed up to send you upstairs in a hurry." Jubal hoped he had gotten the name right. He didn't want any slip-ups now.

114

"Tom hurt? What happened?"

"I don't know. They just said for you to hurry. You go on. Don't worry about Miss Blair. I will open the door for her and help her off with her shawl."

Bolt dashed across the porch, leaving Valerie in the care of the doorman.

Jubal Naylor took a deep breath. Bolt had bought his story. By the time he ran to the upstairs bedroom and back down, Jubal would be long gone. He would have Valerie with him at last.

Bolt reached for the door, pulled it open and went into the foyer. The orchestra music filled the empty lobby, softened only by the Oriental carpet. As he started to go into the ballroom, he saw how crowded it was. He wondered if there was another way to reach the upstairs bedroom without going through the ballroom. He moved back across the foyer, looked around to see if there was another door that might lead upstairs.

As he stood there, he heard a muffled scream. At first he thought the scream had come from the ballroom. He heard the scream again, couldn't tell if it was coming from upstairs or from outside. Outside! Valerie! The doorman! Suddenly it dawned on him that the man he had just talked to wasn't the same doorman who had let them out when they left about an hour ago.

For the second time that night, he wished he had worn his pistol.

He dashed out the front door just in time to see the uniformed man run around the corner of the building, dragging Valerie with him.

Bolt took the steps three at a time, ran around the

corner, darted across the lawn after them. He chased them until they disappeared into the dark night. He ran faster, trying to catch up with them before they were gone for good.

Valerie screamed again. It gave him a sense of direction. He ran as fast as he could, his side aching. He couldn't see them at all, even though the moon was bright. There were too many trees on the landscape, too many bushes and flowers.

Finally, he stopped, listened with a keen ear. He couldn't hear Valerie's cries or moans. He couldn't even hear their running footsteps anymore. He wouldn't give up. He had to find Valerie, bring her back safely.

The seconds ticked by. He listened. No sounds. His eyes pierced the darkness as he searched for their dark forms. Nothing. The seconds stretched into minutes. He was losing valuable time.

He turned his head slowly, listening carefully. A breeze stirred the branches of the bushes to his left. Or maybe it wasn't the breeze. He looked in that direction, saw nothing but the moon-tipped cypress trees, their gnarled limbs looking like some hideous monster.

Just as he was about to turn in another direction to continue his search, something caught his eye. A flash of white among the dark trees. He stood perfectly still, watched. It moved, seemed to change shape as the darkness played tricks on his eyes.

When it moved again, he knew what it was. Valerie's shawl. It had to be.

Taking one step at a time, moving so he wouldn't make any noise, he inched toward the trees. As he got

116

closer, the scent of Valerie's perfume drifted to his nostrils and he knew for sure that she was there.

He took two more steps. A branch snapped beneath his foot. The sound thundered in his ears, caused his heart to skip a beat.

Jubal jumped out from the tree, swung at Bolt with one arm. Valerie was clutched tight under his other arm.

Bolt dodged the fist, swung around, crashed down on Jubal's head with both hands.

"You dirty bastard!" he screamed as he delivered the blow.

Jubal released his hold on the girl, doubled up a fist and aimed at Bolt's jaw.

Bolt side-stepped, drew his fist up, and connected with Jubal's chin. The man grunted with the pain, staggered backwards. Bolt followed through with another blow to Jubal's face, and then another. Bolt felt the wetness on his hand where the blood had dripped from Jubal's nose.

"Run, Valerie!" he shouted. He turned for just an instant, saw her white shawl ripple as she ran across the grounds toward the house.

Bolt's fist was ready when he turned back. He wanted to pound the shit out of Valerie's attacker. But there was no one there to strike. He heard the heavy footsteps of the doorman as he ran away, disappeared once again into the darkness. It was Bolt's instinct to chase him down, mash him to pulp, but right now he was more concerned with Valerie than about the jasper who had tried to snatch her away.

Bolt turned and ran after Valerie, caught up to her just as she reached the steps. He grabbed her, held her in his arms until she had caught her breath.

"I'm so sorry, Valerie," he said. He felt her body quiver in his arms.

"Not your fault," she said, her breath still coming in short gulps.

"I shouldn't have left you alone. When I saw that it was a different doorman, I should have known something was wrong."

"I didn't think anything about it. I don't know why you should have. The servants who are here tonight were just hired for this special event. All but the dozen permanent employees. They change all around during the evening, so you never know who's where."

"Did you know that doorman?"

"No. I've never seen him before."

"Can't say as I blame him for wanting to cart you away. I'd do the same thing if I had the chance. You hurt?"

"No. If my knees would stop shaking, I'd be good as new. What can I say now? You've saved my life again. Twice in two days. 'Thank you' doesn't seem enough."

"Knowing you're safe is enough." He gave her a squeeze.

"I guess we'd better get back inside before my father finds out we didn't take Bing Chee with us."

"I don't need any more trouble tonight," Bolt sighed.

"Bolt, please don't tell anybody about this."

"Do I look like I kiss and tell?"

"I didn't mean that, silly. I meant, don't tell anybody about the doorman. I don't want to spoil the evening."

"This is something that can't be kept to yourself. I think it ought to be kept quiet but there are some who should know about it. Your father, for one. I want him to be aware that someone was trying to kidnap you so he can keep an eye on you for a couple of days."

"You make it sound so serious. He was a creep. He was scared, too, or he wouldn't have run away from you. He'll never show his face again. It was an isolated incident. I can't hide out and have my father protecting me the rest of my life."

Bolt didn't want to tell her that he suspected that someone had tried to kidnap her the day of the fire. For all he knew, they could be the same person.

"Just for a couple of days. Trust me."

"I trust you. But don't tell anyone else. Especially my mother. She'd never let me go out in public again if she found out. She worries too much about me as it is."

"If you were my daughter, I'd worry about you, too. You ready to go back in?"

"Do I look all right?"

"You look like you've lost your cherry, but other than that, you look the same."

"Bolt, you're terrible." She pounded her fist on his arm.

"Would you like a drink?" Bolt asked when they got inside the ballroom.

"I could use one."

"I see your folks over there. Why don't you go over and join them while I get the drinks. They're probably wondering about you. And don't worry about telling your father right now. I'll talk to him later."

Bolt went over to the bar when Valerie walked away. He ordered two whiskeys.

"Oh, you're back," said the bartender.

"Didn't know you cared that much."

"I heard about you sneaking out of here with that pretty Blair gal."

"What do you mean, sneaking out? Everybody saw us leave."

"Not the doorman.

"What the hell are you talking about?"

"I was talking to the doorman a while ago and he said he didn't see you leave."

"Hell, he opened the door for us."

"Said he was taking a leak about the time you left."

"Was he asking about us?"

"Asked where Valerie was. Her parents were at the table at the time and we got to talking about Valerie after they left. That's all."

"You know who it was?"

"Think his name's Joe. At least that's the name of one of the doormen."

"Are there more than one?"

"Who knows around here. All of us are new and we just work where they tell us to. We spell each other, change around, you know."

"Thanks for the drinks." Bolt headed for Valerie and her parents. He was beginning to get an inkling of what had happened outside with the doorman. He got a sick feeling in the pit of his stomach when he thought about it.

It had been a set up from the beginning. It was no

isolated incident as Valerie chose to believe. Someone was out to get her. And that someone was still on the loose.

Chapter Twelve

Annabelle Snyder noticed when Bolt and Valerie walked in the door. Her eyes flashed with jealousy. She had a good idea what they had been up to and it didn't surprise her a bit. Valerie always pretended to be so pure, but the two girls were the same age and Annabelle knew that Valerie must be experiencing the same sexual arousals that she herself felt. Whether they liked to admit it or not, all girls wanted to know what it was like to sleep with a man. Annabelle had tried it and liked it from the beginning and she saw no harm in taking pleasure as it came.

She liked the way Bolt walked, the way he threw his chest out when he strolled across the floor like he knew what he was going after. Not like the men she was used to seeing who walked stiffly, like they were about to shit their britches. She liked the way he wore his hair. Long by the standards of her friends, but it looked good on him. And his smile. The way his lips curled to the side when he smiled sent shivers down her spine. She would do anything to spend one night

ith him, to have him look at her with those pale blue
yes, to feel the bulge between his legs.

"Hello, Bolt," she said as he carried the two drinks
cross the dance floor. "I wondered when you and
'alerie would get back. You still owe me a dance, you
now."

"There's no music right now," he said.

"I could hum a tune."

"You could, but I'm busy right now."

"I can wait."

"Good. I'll see you later, then."

"You sure will."

Bolt walked away from her, joined Valerie and her
arents. When he found the opportunity, he took
Rodney Blair aside and told him about the incident
vith the doorman. He didn't tell him that he sus-
ected that someone had tried to kidnap Valerie the
ay before.

"Seems you're making a habit of saving my
aughter's life. I'm glad you were there," Blair said.

"I didn't want to worry you," Bolt said, "but I
hink it would be a good idea to keep Valerie at home
or a couple of days. Just to be sure."

"We're going to have to be more careful about the
elp we hire for these big parties. With all the em-
loyees we hired for tonight, I guess we were bound
o get an unstable one in the bunch. I'll keep Valerie
n for a few days."

Bolt finally danced with Annabelle Snyder and was
glad when it was over. He spotted Tom a little later
nd was on his way over to talk to him when Mister
Snyder stopped him and invited him to supper the
ollowing evening. Bolt thought about it for a minute,

then remembered his appointment with Jewel.

"I'm sorry, I already have plans for tomorro
night."

"We'll make it for dinner at noon, then," Snyde
insisted.

Bolt agreed and he and Tom stayed at the part
until after the midnight supper was served. They sai
goodnight to everyone, headed for the door. Th
doorman had the door open for them by the time the
got there. It was the same doorman who had let the
in when they first arrived.

"Did someone spell you for a while this evening?"
Bolt asked him.

"Yep. A man can't be expected to stand in th
same place all evening long without a little relie
Even doormen have to shake the dew from their lil
once in a while."

"Did just one man spell you?"

"No. There were two different ones. One early o
in the evening and the other one about fiftee
minutes ago when they were serving the food."

"Did you know either one of them?"

"One of them I did. The other one, I never lai
eyes on before."

"Which one did you know?"

"The early-on one. Jubal Naylor. Everyone know
who Naylor is. Surprised me, though. I thought h
was out back watchin' over his gals, but they must
been short-handed tonight 'cause he said he was sen
to spell me. Hell, I don't care who watches the door.
ain't about to turn down a chance to get off my feet."

"Think Naylor's still out back?"

"No. Them gals were taken before the food wa

served. I seen 'em go. But it wasn't Jubal who took 'em. It was one of his strong arms.''

"Thanks." Bolt dug five bucks out of his pocket and handed it to the doorman.

On the way out to their horses, Bolt thought about his appointment with Jewel the next night. He wouldn't dare show up. Jubal Naylor knew what he looked like and if Jubal saw Bolt visiting Jewel, he might put two and two together and come up with a loaded pistol.

"Tom, I got a favor to . . .''

"Don't go any further. The answer's no."

"But you haven't even heard what I want you to do yet."

"The answer's still no. I've done favors for you before."

"Let's put it this way. How would you like to visit the House of Paradise tomorrow night?''

"Visit or patronize?"

"I knew I'd get your attention."

"You got a hundred bucks to throw down on it?''

"I'll pay."

"I'll go."

The next morning, Bolt decided not to wait until Merle Stamps paid him a visit. He wanted answers right away. If they pooled their information, maybe they could stop Naylor and the kidnap ring before anyone else got hurt.

Stamps was reluctant to talk to Bolt at first.

"I don't want to steal your damned story, Stamps. I want to see if you know who's at the bottom of all this. From what I can gather, the House of Paradise is just a front for the kidnap ring. Naylor's up to his neck in it, but he's taking orders from someone else. I want to know who."

"I think I've got it figured out. My boss, Charles De Young, thinks it's Mayor Kalloch because we found out about all his dirty dealings in Kansas. He's a con man, clear to the bone. That's for sure. But he's not involved with the kidnap ring any more than the other men who use the services of the girls. Last night I pressured him into telling me a lot of inside stuff. Told him he had a choice. If he gave me the information I wanted, I'd do a favorable story about him. Otherwise, I'd crucify him in the paper. He knew I could do it, too, because I showed him some of the clippings I had from the Kansas papers. Kalloch admitted that he knew about the kidnapping of society girls from other parts of the country, and said that he had agreed to look the other way, give the kidnappers a free hand in the city as long as he was supplied with girls whenever he wanted them. He said he made that deal with Jubal but that Jubal was only acting on orders from a Chinaman."

"I've heard about a Chinaman, too," Bolt said.

"Kalloch swore up and down that he didn't know who the Chinaman was and I believe him."

"What about Emory Howes, the bank employee? He took us out back last night and he seemed to know the whole routine."

"Naw. Howes hasn't got the brains to run an operation like that. I know he's friendly with Jubal, but then he's friendly with everyone. But Howes might be more involved than we think. I hear Blair has ordered an audit of his books. Seems there's

126

some missing funds that can't be accounted for. I'm not saying Howes has anything to do with that, but it does seem odd that Blair has never had any trouble at his bank before. Howes is his newest employee, you know."

"Then who do you think it is?"

"Woo Fong. You met him last night. He's the only one above suspicion."

"And that makes him guilty?"

"It's just a theory at this point. I always take the opposite end of the stick on these things. Start with the most innocent man and work my way down to the most probable culprit. Nine times out of ten, my theories prove out."

"Hell of a thing to base a verdict on."

"Well, he is a Chinaman. At least that fits."

Bolt shook his head.

"I've got something else I'd like to throw at you. What about Valerie Blair? I think someone tried to kidnap her the day of the fire, but I can't prove it."

"And you think Gimpy was the one."

"How'd you know?"

"I got the news of the fire right away. You were too busy to notice me, but I was there. I saw Gimpy hanging around. He kept track of Valerie the whole time. When I heard about his death, I knew he had money. And Gimpy never had money unless he was working. Lately, he's worked mostly for Jubal. Makes sense. Jubal hired Gimpy to kidnap Valerie."

"Jubal attempted another kidnap last night at the Ball. I was witness to that."

"I know. I heard about it."

"You don't miss a bet, do you?"

"I got eyes and ears, same as everyone else."

"But why would Jubal want to kidnap Valerie? She's a local girl and from what I can tell, all of the other girls are from other places."

"Maybe he's got a hard-on for her."

"You make everything sound so easy, but I'm confused."

"Here's something else for you. I think there's going to be another shipment of girls coming in tonight, by boat, just before dark. And I know for sure there's a stage coming in tomorrow morning that's full of beautiful girls. Whether they're part of the same deal, I don't know, but they're on their way. I think you can find Woo Fong at either place because I know the head honcho meets each shipment to make a head count before he pays off the delivery boys. When I talked to Woo Fong last night under the pretense of doing a story, I learned that he would be indisposed at the very times the shipments of girls are due."

"I must say, you've done your homework. I'll be in touch with you before tonight if I have anything new to report. I assume you're going to be at the boat dock tonight." Bolt got up to leave.

"Yes. I need an ending for my story."

"I'll see you then if not before."

"Before you go, I'd like to thank you for saving Valerie's life. She's very special to me. I guess I've been in love with her since the first time I saw her, but I'm not allowed to court her because of my lowly station in life."

"If it means anything, in my book, you've got the rest of the assholes beat by a mile."

* * *

Bolt cursed himself all the way out to the Snyder ranch for agreeing to have dinner with them. He hated being locked in to appointments. He already missed the open trail where there were no places he had to be, no appointed times to be there. He knew the city life was changing him, making him soft. Human beings were pretty damned adaptable. They tended to blend into any environment they were in, take on the qualities of its people. Last night's party had showed him a great deal. He found himself conforming to the rich people's society. He wore their damned monkey suit, danced their dances, watched his language so he wouldn't offend some doddering fool, held the stomach gas in when he wanted to let it rip without having to say excuse me. He even listened to endless conversations about nothing that mattered to him.

Some people found the big cities more exciting, but to him, all cities were the same. People had their fights over property lines and water rights. People dressed to please each other instead of themselves. Life was supposed to be easier in the big cities, but as far as he was concerned, it was harder. There were more places to go, more things to do, a constant busyness just to have more time. He preferred the simple life where a man could wash in the stream, piss on the ground, roll a sleeping bag out at night to sleep under the stars and own the land for a brief time just because he was there.

Bolt had only been in San Francisco two days and already he was caught up in the whirlwind of that society. Maybe Tom was right. Pay for a piece of ass and be done with it. No strings, no involvement and no damned appointments.

By the time he got to Annabelle's ranch, he was not in a very good mood. He took a deep breath, tried to change his mood. He glanced around him, was glad for the open spaces around the estate. The Snyders lived out in the country where they could raise their horses and even the smell of hay and horse dung felt good to him. There were no other houses in sight, except for a small cottage out back and several out buildings that were needed for the stock. The place reminded him of a ranch out in Arizona that he loved so much and almost bought, but the Snyder house was much more elaborate. It was good to be out in the country again where the worries blew away like dried tumbleweeds snatched from their home in the ground to travel with the whimsy of the breezes. Already, Bolt felt much better.

Annabelle was waiting on the front porch for him. She waved when she saw him, then ran out to greet him.

"You're right on time," she said. "Mother's planned a special dinner for you and it will be served in ten minutes. We always eat at noon. Come on in and get washed up. After dinner, I'll show you around the grounds."

"Don't you ever get tired of always eating at noon?"

"Of course not. It's always been that way."

"Nice place you've got here."

"Daddy raises race horses. I know you'll want to see them. I'll take you for a nice long walk. Or maybe you'd like to go riding. I've set aside the whole afternoon for entertaining you."

"I can't stay very long, Annabelle. I've got a lot to do in town."

"Oh, you'll stay. I'll make it worth your while." She thrust her breasts up, ran her tongue across her lips.

"You're pretty bold, aren't you?"

"I know what I want. And I usually get what I want."

"Well, this time might be the exception."

"Not when it's something I want so bad."

Chapter Thirteen

There was something that bothered Bolt about the Snyder household. Although he was treated royally by the Snyders and their help, he felt uncomfortable. He was waited on constantly, every want satisfied. The food was good, the wines and liquors the best, the service and attention outstanding. But still the feeling was there. He knew what it was. The atmosphere in the house was not comfortable. He sensed a stiffness, an uneasiness that had not been present at the Blair home.

Even the Chinese servants and maids did not seem happy. They did their jobs, and did them well, but they did not relax and talk with him as Bing Chee had.

Bolt watched their faces as they served the after-dinner drinks in the large living room. They did not smile or make eye contact. The maid who served coffee for the two women disappeared as soon as she poured the drinks. The Chinese boy took up his place in the corner of the room when he was through, waiting to fulfill any needs that might arise. Bolt sat facing the boy and although he entered in the conversation, Bolt couldn't keep his eyes off the boy who was called Chin. The boy stared straight ahead and his gaze fell directly over Bolt's head which gave Bolt the eerie feeling at times that Chin was staring directly at him.

Bolt talked to Snyder about his race horses, but he looked up at Chin every time he felt the boy's eyes on him. Each time, Chin's eyes were focused above Bolt's head. It took Bolt several minutes to notice the bruise on the boy's neck, but when he did, it startled him. He had seen too many bruises lately.

After he noticed the bruise, he found it impossible to concentrate on the conversation. He found himself wondering about the boy. He was younger than most servants, probably sixteen or seventeen, a time of his life when he should be happy and thinking about girls his own age. Maybe he had to work to support his parents.

"You ready to take that ride?" Annabelle said when the conversation fell flat.

Bolt wanted to beg off, but he didn't.

"Yes. A short ride."

"We've got a big place here. It might take a while." Her eyes drilled into Bolt's. She wet her lips with her tongue again, formed a small "O" with her moist lips.

Bolt recognized a brazen proposition when he saw one and this girl made no attempt to conceal it from her mother and father. Were her parents so wrapped up in their own social importance that they could not see it for themselves? Were they so out of tune with reality that they had forgotten what it was like to be young and horny? Maybe that was the way girls in the big city acted, but in the small towns where he was from, a girl like Annabelle would be scorned by the townspeople for such boldness.

"Give me a minute to change into my riding breeches," she said. She got up from her chair, walked away from him, her buttocks thrust high in the air.

Bolt glanced over at the Chinese boy, saw that he was still staring over Bolt's head. Bolt wondered if he had noticed her boldness. His eyes fell to the bruise on the boy's neck and he wondered about that, too.

"Mind if Chin shows me your horses while I'm waiting for Annabelle?" Bolt asked.

"Not at all. I'm proud of those horses. I've got two winners out there. They bring in a lot of money. We're already training the others and they'll be winners, too. With what I've made on selling some of them and putting them up for stud, they keep my finances up with the best of them."

Bolt had no use for people who bragged about their money. In fact that was one of the things that jarred him about the guests at the party the night before. Not that they bragged about their money, but they judged each other's success by how much money they had, how many diamonds in the women's brooches. He felt sorry for them in a way.

Out on the open trail, there were times when Bolt felt like he owned everything when he owned nothing at all. But here in the city it was just the opposite. He had a lot of the money in the bank, the promise of owning valuable property and yet he felt like he had nothing. He didn't have his freedom and that was what success was all about.

"Yes, I'd like to see your show horses," Bolt said.

"Not show horses," Snyder corrected. "Race horses. There's a difference, you know. And I can count the difference all the way to the bank. Chin, take Mister Bolt out to the stables and show him my two money makers."

Without looking at anyone, Chin turned and walked toward the side door, expecting Bolt to follow him.

No words were exchanged during the long walk out to the stables. Once there, Chin announced the names of the two horses then stepped back and stood at attention while Bolt looked at the horses. After Bolt admired the horses, he stepped back, stood next to Chin and tried to engage the boy in conversation.

"Nice horses. Do you ride them?"

"No."

"Do you train them?"

"No."

"Do you help take care of them? Feed them or brush them?"

"No. That is not my job."

"What do you do here, Chin?"

"I work in the house. I take care of Master."

"Master? Is that what you call him?"

"That what he is."

"What about the girl? What does she do?"

"She serve the lady. That all she do. She work velly hard."

"Are there any other workers here?"

"Yes. Many servants. All have own job to do."

"Chin, how did you get that bruise on your neck?"

For the first time, the Chinese boy looked at Bolt. He didn't speak for a long time.

"I fall down the stairs."

"Do you have any family in San Francisco?"

"My sister. That my sister you meet. She work velly hard."

"What about your parents?"

"They velly far away."

"Where do they live?"

Again the boy looked at Bolt.

"I do not tell you."

"Do they know you're here?"

"They know I am gone from them."

"Do you like working here, Chin? Does your sister?"

"We do our work. We do not complain."

Bolt knew he was getting nowhere with the boy. He wanted to find out if the girl had been kidnapped and now, since learning she was Chin's sister, he wondered if they had both been taken from their home and brought to the Barbary Coast by the same outfit Jubal was connected with.

"Must be nice to work for wealthy people," Bolt said, changing his tactics. "How much do you earn?"

"We get food. We get clothes. We get bed. No more. The Master say he already pay too much for us when he buy us."

"He bought you? That's slavery, Chin."

"We do not think of it that way."

"Were you kidnapped? You and your sister? The others?"

Chin looked at Bolt again. This time he did not look away.

"Yes. We are taken from our home. We do not want to go. We come here and we must do what we are told. Sometimes not easy. Even the girl, Miss Annabelle, she order me to go to the cottage with her when parents are away. She make me do things I do not want to do."

"You are afraid to tell me these things, aren't you?"

"Yes. I will get beat if the Master find out. He kick me down the stairs. That how I get hurt." Chin was still looking at Bolt.

"Why are you telling me now?"

"It is my sister. She cry every night to see our mother and father. She cry for other reasons, too. I know the Master has his way with her sometimes. She does not tell me these things. I can see it for myself one day. I can no longer watch her cry."

"Who did this to you? Who kidnapped you?"

"I do not tell you that."

"It's important, Chin. For your sister's sake, please tell me. I can help you."

"One of my own kind did this to us. That is all I tell you."

"Was it a man named Woo Fong?"

Chin jerked his head around, stared again straight ahead of him.

"I tell you too much already. I tell you no more."

Bolt walked over and patted one of the horses on the nose. From Chin's reaction when he mentioned Woo Fong's name, Bolt was beginning to think Merle Stamps was right about the Chinaman.

"Like our horses?" said the voice behind him. Bolt didn't have to turn around to know that it was Annabelle. He could smell her perfume even before she stepped up to him and slipped her arm through his. When he looked at her, he was startled by the outfit she was wearing. Tight brown riding breeches. A matching jacket with nothing on underneath it. Only the bottom button was fastened. Her over-sized breasts were fully exposed, the nipples hardened from the exposure.

"Yes. They look like they could win a race or two."

"Chin, my father wants you back in the house now."

The boy walked away without speaking.

"Where'd your father get his servants? Chin seems like a nice quiet boy?" Bolt asked.

"Daddy bought them at the auction," she said with no hesitation.

"I thought they only sold slaves at auctions."

"Oh, no. Good help is hard to find and we all know you have to pay a lot of money these days to get a good worker. Whoever can pay the most money gets the best workers. It's that simple."

"Who gets the money?"

Annabelle shrugged her shoulders. "I don't know. I never paid that much attention to it. Come on. I have a special hideaway I want to show you."

Bolt forgot about his troubles as they rode across the open fields. He felt better than he had in days with the wind beating against his face. He didn't even mind Annabelle's boldness now. In fact, he found it refreshing to be with her. At least she was honest about what she wanted. Not like some of the other girls he'd met who pretended to be shy and innocent, or the ones who teased a man to death and then wouldn't put out. He felt comfortable with Annabelle. He knew he could use any language he wanted to with her and she'd never bat an eye.

She rode ahead of him now, leading the way. He watched her bottom bounce up and down, slap against the saddle. He imagined her bare breasts bobbing up and down, the breeze keeping her nipples hard. He had heard that some girls got their rocks off by the constant vibrating pressure against their pussies when they rode a horse. He'd have to ask Annabelle about it. If anyone could, she would be the one.

He tipped his head back, let the sun drench his pores. They jumped a rabbit and he felt like he was on the open trail again. He scanned the countryside, saw no buildings, no streets, no people. He had his freedom back and that was all he needed.

They rode through a stand of pines, went up an incline. When they reached the top, the ocean was spread out before them like a cool green blanket. Annabelle reined up on her horse.

"This is it." She climbed down from her horse, began stripping out of her clothes right away.

"You get right down to it, don't you?"

"Take your clothes off and drape them over your saddle. We're gonna go for a swim first."

"And then what?" he teased.

"Then you're gonna fuck the living hell out of me."

When they were both naked, she grabbed a blanket

from her saddlehorn, threw it over her shoulder. They ran down the hill, across the sand. She spread the blanket on the ground, jumped into the water. Bolt's knob, which had started to rise, shriveled up into a mass of flesh when he hit the cold water.

"Don't worry about your pecker," she said. "I'll bring it back to life."

"At least the water should cool down that hot pussy of yours for a while."

"Not a chance. I'm always hot. Don't you hear the water sizzling?"

"You're some kind of gal."

"Hell, why beat around the bush? I want it, I say so. If you don't want it, tell me. No hard feelings that way."

"You talk too much." He waded over to her, grabbed a breast and kissed her hard on the lips. Beneath the water he felt her hand reach for his withered cock. She toyed with it until it began to swell again.

"One quick swim to get the blood stirring, then I'll race you to shore." She dove into the water and swam away from him.

Five minutes later she climbed out of the water just ahead of him, water dripping from the hairs between her legs. As Bolt looked at her large breasts, her slim waistline, he felt a tug at his manhood. He took her in his arms, crushed her to his body. He liked the feel of her cool wet body against his flesh. He kissed her damp mouth, flicked a tongue deep inside. His cock pulsed and stiffened, jabbed into her warming body. He felt her hand at his crotch as she found his shaft and squeezed it.

"You're spoiling my fun," she said when they broke the kiss. "I wanted to suck you up a little."

"Nobody's stopping you."

They tumbled onto the blanket and she quickly moved her head over his cock. She sucked hard, running her hand up and down the veined length. Bolt raised his head, glanced down and saw his glistening cock going in and out of her mouth, her cheeks hollow from the pressure.

He thrust his loins up in the air, pushed her head down tight against his crotch. It was almost a mistake. He almost spilled his seed inside her mouth.

"Roll over and spread 'em, baby. You're gonna get about six inches of turkey neck dumped in your slot."

He sank his shaft into her slippery pussy, felt it tighten around him. He jammed it to the bottom of her well, drew it out to the flared tip then drove it home again.

"Fuck me, fuck me good," she shouted in his ear. But he didn't hear her. He blotted out everything except the pulsing pleasure in his hard stiff cock. He pounded it into her again and again until he shot his wad deep inside the hot gripping pussy.

"What are you doing in San Francisco?" she asked when they were dressing.

"Looking for a place to open a business."

"I have a friend who owns a lot of property. Maybe I can help you find something. What kind of business are you in?"

"Whorehouses. I own a string of 'em across the West."

She stopped where she was, her riding breeches,

half way up her legs. She looked at his face, expecting him to laugh.

"You're not kidding, are you?"

"No. It's true."

"Well, I'll be damned." She pulled her pants all the way up, fastened the buttons. "What a job to have. No wonder you're so good in the sack. You've got all that pussy to keep you in practice."

"I don't diddle my own girls. Rule one."

"Bullshit. Never knew a man yet who didn't take advantage of a woman."

"Believe what you want to but I don't need to fuck with them. I've never had any trouble finding a horny twat when I wanted one. I found you, didn't I?"

"I think it was the other way around. I was the one who dragged you out here for a piece of ass."

"See what I mean?"

"I'll bet you make a lot of money. Not much overhead in running a whorehouse once you've bought your whores and paid for your building. The rest should be straight profit."

"I make enough. But I don't buy my girls. If they want to work for me fine. If they don't, there's plenty of others who do. I pay 'em a good salary."

"How much? About two percent of your profits?"

"No. I pay them a flat salary, once a week."

"No matter how many men they service?"

"No matter. Even when there's no business, they get paid. If they work for me, they get paid to look nice, keep themselves clean and to be ready when they're needed."

"That's dumb. You give them a place to stay, food, I assume. They couldn't need many clothes in that line of work. What else could they need?"

"Dignity."

Bolt didn't think she would understand why a whore needed dignity. And if she couldn't understand that, then she would not know that he was comparing the whores to what her father was doing to the Chinese servants by keeping them as slaves.

But he felt a hell of a lot better for saying it.

Chapter Fourteen

When Bolt returned from Annabelle Snyder's home, he followed the shoreline of the Barbary Coast, his horse ankle deep in the water. He knew that the small boat that brought Penny to the shore two days before had docked somewhere near the Pelican Point Hotel, but out of sight of the hotel. Penny had told him that she had been taken by wagon to the bordello, so he was searching for a spot along the coastline that would be easily accessible to both boat and buggy and yet not visible by anyone on land.

It didn't take him long to find the spot since the wagon wheel tracks that led away from the hidden cove were still fresh in the damp sand. The cove was midway between the Shorecliff Club and the Pelican Point Hotel. A high bluff hid the cove so it could not be seen from either place.

He followed the tracks that went along the coastline for a brief time, then went up a slight incline before hey traveled on the floor between two high cliffs. The racks ended up on the road that led away from the Shorecliff Club where they were lost to the carriage racks from the party the night before.

At that point, Bolt turned his horse, Nick, back oward the Shorecliff Club. He rode the horse up to he edge of the high cliff that was on property belonging to the Club. When he looked over the edge, ae could see the ocean, part of the hidden cove. But it wasn't good enough. He needed a spot where he could see the whole cove.

He dismounted, walked along the edge of the cliff until he found a place where it wasn't so steep. He climbed down a few feet, sat on a small ledge that protruded from the cliff wall. It was perfect. From there he could see the entire cove and the ocean without moving from spot to spot. It would work to his advantage because if anyone happened to look in his direction, he was too far away to be recognized and yet it would not be an unlikely place for a club member to sit and watch the ocean.

Tom was waiting for him when he got back to the hotel. The two of them rode into town where Bolt bought a pair of field glasses and a pair of light colored work pants that would blend in with the rock bluff, a matching shirt.

While they were eating an early supper, Bolt gave Tom the hundred dollars for his visit to the House of Paradise.

"This city life's the greatest, isn't it?" Tom grinned as he stuffed the money in his pocket. "Big stores where a man can buy some decent clothes, a variety of nice restaurants where you can order food from different countries, all that cultural stuff. And no more dusty cattle trails."

"Those trails taught us something, Tom. They taught us to be real men. We're getting too soft. At least when we rode the cattle trails we were tough as boot heels. I'll bet neither one of us could lift half the weight we used to when we were handling those grain barrels."

"Yeah, we've gone the hard road together and it was a hell of a lot of fun. I kinda miss that life."

"When I was out at Annabelle's place today, I got itchy to be on the trail again."

"Is that all you got itchy for?"

"Hell, she's a fuckin' tiger. It wasn't a wasted trip by any means. The only thing that spoiled the day was all their goddamn talk about money. All three of them. Even Annabelle got on my ass because I pay my whores to work for me. Do you know that they've actually got slaves working for them out there? Brought in along with Naylor's whores, I'm sure. Or maybe some of them were Naylor's kidnapped whores before they were turned out to pasture. It's criminal what he's doing. There's high society for you. I prefer the good old country folk."

"Shouldn't he be reported?"

"When we're through with all this mess, I think there are going to be a lot of rich asses in a sling. But I'm not going to rock the boat until every damn one of those girls is free. If Jubal and the Chinaman are selling the girls for slaves, we'll probably never find all of them. But at least we'll free the ones that we can."

"I think we opened Pandora's box when you

saved Valerie's life. This thing's snowballed all to hell."

"You know what scares me?" Bolt said. "Sometimes I think I'm getting to be just like them. I've been thinking too much about money lately. I'm thinking bigger whorehouses, a home overlooking the ocean, things that cost a lot of greenbacks. If I plunk all my money down, we'll be tied down to one place. That's not what I want."

"No. I wouldn't want to be stuck in one place the rest of my life."

"Most people are. And they don't even know the difference. Don't lose that money I gave you. I shudder every time I think about that three thousand I gave you to keep for me."

"I don't want to hear about it again. That must be our favorite story."

"Be sure you get Jewel," he said, "even if you have to say that you tried her out at the party last night and wanted more. She may not have been able to get the information, but if she did, she'll tell you the name of the Chinaman who is at the head of the kidnap ring. If things go like I hope they will for me tonight, I may be able to find out for myself. Tell her that I already found out that there will be a load of girls coming in by boat this evening, another load of girls due in here by stage in the morning."

"Do I tell her this before or after she pleasures me?"

"Your brain's in your cock, isn't it? Tell her during. And tell her I apologize for sending you as my replacement."

147

"Hell, she'll be glad you couldn't make it when I get through with her."

"Just so you get my money's worth I don't care. If there's any way you can slip her out of there in your hip pocket, please do it."

"You're serious about that, aren't you?"

"I sure as hell am. I gotta get goin'. By the time I go back to the hotel and change clothes, it'll be time to head over to the bluffs."

"Be careful, Bolt. If you're thinking about going back on the trail, you don't need a bunch of broken bones."

The ship was a mere pinpoint on flat surface of the water, even through the field glasses Bolt had purchased that afternoon. He sat on the small ledge, high on the hilltop where he could watch the ship when it came closer to shore. The sun could be a problem. It was high above the horizon, but if the ship crossed its path when it dipped lower, he wouldn't be able to track the ship. It would be another hour before the sun slipped out of sight.

Merle Stamps sat on the bluff some ten feet above him. He couldn't see more than half of the hidden cove, but he didn't need to. He and Bolt had a plan. Both men were armed.

The rumbling of wagon wheels alerted them that someone was coming. Bolt sat perfectly still, listening to the creak of the wheels. He knew when the wagon was passing through the miniature canyon between the two cliffs. When it emerged from the narrow passageway, he glanced down, saw that the wagon was covered. He trained his field glasses on the rig, but as the buggy turned right, the driver was hidden behind the heavy cloth covering.

The wheels creaked along the path until the wagon was tucked back into the far recesses of the cove. Through the glasses, Bolt watched the driver climb down from the seat, walk around to the back where he used his size and strength to pull a small boat from the floor of the covered wagon. As the big man turned around to set the boat down on the sandy beach, Bolt got a good look at his face. He didn't recognize it, but he would if he ever saw it again.

There had been two boats the day Bolt had watched from his hotel window. He figured there would be two today. The driver stepped up to the wagon again and Bolt waited for him to pull another boat out. Instead, the man pulled out a set of oars, attached them to the boat.

Bolt looked up at Stamps, held up one finger. It was the signal that only one rescue boat was being used.

The man below slid the boat across the sand, shoved it into the water and climbed in. A minute later, he was well into the water, rowing toward the sailing vessel which was coming close enough to be recognized as a ship.

From his position on the top of the bluff, Stamps could see the front of the cove. When he saw the boat in the water, he knew it was time for him to make his move. He ran away from the edge of the cliff, followed the path that led through the valley below, dashed up to the wagon. He knew his timing was critical. If anyone else showed up while he was down there, he'd be trapped. There was only one way out and that was the path between the two bluffs.

He drew a small saw out of his jacket, set to work hacking through the spokes of the front wheels. He didn't need to saw through all of them. Just enough so the front of the wagon would collapse to the ground when it was moved.

Bolt cursed the sun as it slid down behind the big ship which was closer than it had been before. He lost track of both boats in the blinding sun but he knew that it would not take the small boat very long to return with its load. He turned the glasses toward the cove, watched Stamps saw through the spokes.

Stamps got out of there just in time. By the time Bolt spotted the boat again, it was only ten feet offshore.

The boat eased into the shoreline and the big man stepped out, held it in place with a rope as the girls got out one at a time. Peering through the field glasses, Bolt got a good look at all of the girls. He saw the hogleg that was strapped to the driver's leg.

Bolt scurried up to the top of the bluff, ran across the field. He took up his position at the entranceway to the narrow canyon. Stamps stood at the other side. There was no way the driver could get by them.

Bolt was disappointed that the Chinaman had not come to make the head count, but maybe with so few girls it was not necessary. When they heard the loud snap of the wagon crashing to the ground, Bolt and Stamps drew their pistols and waited.

Finally they heard the voices as the group entered the other end of the canyon.

"Keep it moving, bitches," snarled the driver.

One girl screamed when he cracked her across the shoulders because she wasn't moving fast enough to suit him. The other girls gasped, screeched, moaned.

"Shut up you filthy whores or you'll have a face that even your own mother wouldn't recognize."

They were getting closer.

"We're gonna have to walk to town, so from here on it's up to you whether you live or die. When we get closer to town we're gonna be meetin' up with some townfolk. I don't want no funny stuff. I want you to walk in front of me in lines, two across. If any of you try to escape or talk to anyone, I'll blow you away without thinking twice about it. You understand?"

The girls answered in whispered voices.

"Now line up and keep it movin'."

A minute later the first two girls moved into sight. Bolt and Stamps moved back so they wouldn't see them. It was going easier than Bolt had expected. All of the girls would clear the entranceway and be out of danger by the time the driver came through.

Two more girls filed by.

"When you get to town, you'd better not look scared," the loud voice boomed.

After the last two girls went by, Bolt moved closer to the entrance, his gun cocked and poised.

The driver emerged with his hogleg aimed at the back of the girls' heads. Bolt hadn't counted on that.

As the big man went by, Bolt slid in behind him.

"Hold it right there," he called.

The driver swung around, his pistol already aimed. He squeezed the trigger as soon as he had Bolt in view.

Bolt ducked, fired his own pistol when he realized what was happening.

The driver's aim was high. The bullet skimmed over the top of Bolt's head.

An instant later, Bolt's bullet crashed into the driver's chest. A scream echoed through the miniature canyon as the wounded man crumpled to the ground, the pistol tossed aside when he clutched at his chest. Blood gushed from the hole, stained the shirt in a crimson circle. Pink foam bubbled out of his mouth from the lung wound.

Bolt moved over the man, pressed his pistol against the driver's forehead.

"Who's your boss? The Chinaman. What's his name?" Bolt jammed the barrel into the flesh, slid it down so it was on the bridge of the nose, centered between the man's eyes.

The driver groaned, tried to speak. His voice was a hushed gurgle.

"Louder."

"Woooo Fo-on," was the muffled reply.

Bolt moved away from the dying man, holstered his pistol.

The driver's head fell to his shoulder, his eyes glazed with death.

"It's all over with, girls. At least for you. We'll take you into town and get you back to your homes as soon as we can arrange it."

Stamps walked over and looked at the body.

"Too bad he had to die. Just hope this is the beginning of the end."

"Looks like you were right," Bolt said. "And now we're facing the hardest task of all. We have to see that Jubal Naylor and Woo Fong are stopped before anyone else dies."

Chapter Fifteen

Jubal Naylor paced the floor of his office, too nervous to sit down. He dug the gold watch out of his pocket with two fingers and checked the time again. It was almost eight o'clock and Hogg should have been back with the six new girls two hours ago. Jubal knew he should have sent Carl along to help him, but Hogg said he could handle that many girls by himself.

About a half hour ago, the tension became too much for him. He had sent Carl to look for Hogg and the six girls who would become his whores. He would keep the best of the lot and the others would eventually be sold as maids. Carl hadn't come back either and this only added to his worries.

The mother ship could have had problems and not been able to get close enough to shore for Hogg to pick the girls up in that little boat. Or maybe Hogg had gone out too far in the boat and run into trouble himself. He had gone over the reasons for Hogg's tardiness a dozen times and it still didn't help calm his nerves.

He hoped Hogg got there soon because Woo Fong had ordered a prostitute to be delivered to his home by eight o'clock and Hogg was the only one allowed to make the delivery. Woo Fong insisted that he and Jubal not be seen together so nobody would make the connection that they were involved in business together. Wong didn't visit the whorehouse and he didn't allow Jubal to come to his home. When it was necessary for them to meet, it was always at a secluded house on the edge of town.

Nothing had gone right for Jubal for several days and he was beginning to feel the pressure. Already he had the knot at the back of his head that came only when he was under extreme pressure.

Woo Fong had asked for Jewel tonight and that irritated Jubal. He liked Jewel and considered her his private property. He didn't mind when the customers wanted her because they paid top prices for her and she was the most popular whore he had. But this was different. Woo Fong had no right to her just because he was the boss. Woo Fong could have any girl he wanted. He didn't need her.

Of course, Jubal had no choice in the matter. He didn't have the guts to stand up to Woo Fong. But he'd made sure he had first crack at Jewel. She had spent most of the afternoon with him and he had nearly worn her out with his demands. Let Woo Fong be the one to take seconds.

Jewel had acted strangely today and that had bothered him. She was extremely affectionate with him when it was her nature to be perverse. Most of the time she just lay there and took it, which was worse. She had been talkative, too. Asking a lot of questions. She wasn't pumping him, he knew. Just curious, she said. When she had asked the name of the Chinaman, he had told her Woo Fong's name. It didn't matter. She was going to find out tonight anyway. He didn't care what she knew. She would never leave the bordello.

The thing that bothered him most was not being able to kidnap Valerie Blair. He'd come so close last night with his clever plan. Had her in his arms and halfway to his horse when that damned Bolt showed up and had taken her back. He had to let her go when he'd been caught. Woo Fong was inside attending the party and he didn't want to cause a commotion. He didn't want the Chinaman to know anything about Valerie. He wouldn't give up on her. There'd come a time when she'd be all alone and when he got her he wouldn't share her with Woo Fong.

Bolt had fouled up his plans three times this week. Twice by snatching Valerie just before he could get his hands on her and the other time when he almost got away with Penny. Well, Penny was locked in her room now. She'd not get out again.

Jubal knew what Bolt looked like now. That would come in handy when he took him out. He had to kill him. He couldn't risk having Bolt come to Valerie's rescue again.

Jubal had killed Gimpy that week and hadn't been caught or even suspected so he could do it again.

When Jubal checked his watch again and saw that it was ten minutes before eight, he was frantic. Neither of the men had returned and it was time to take Jewel to Woo Fong's house. The only thing he could do at this late date was to take her himself. He dashed to her room, took her by the arm and headed for the back door.

Just as Jubal reached the back door, he heard the door handle rattle, saw the door begin to open. Jubal was relieved until he saw Carl. Blood dripped from Carl's hands, was spattered on his shirt and trousers.

"What the hell happened to you?" Jubal asked. "Where's Hogg?"

"Hogg's dead."

"Shit. How'd he buy it?"

Carl explained how he had gone to the hidden cove looking for Hogg and found him lying dead at the entrance to the long valley between the bluffs.

"I found the wagon, too, but the fuckin' spokes had been cut. I couldn't even move it. I had to load Hogg's body on my horse which was no easy task considering he weighed over two hundred pounds."

"Got any idea who did it?"

"Hell, no, the fuckin' bastards."

"Wonder if it was someone who knew about the girls or just somebody out for cheap thrills."

"Reckon it don't much matter. Hogg's gone either way."

"Where's the body now?"

"Still draped over my horse. I didn't know what the fuck to do with it. I sure as hell ain't gonna lift it again by myself."

"What about the girls? Where are they?"

"How the fuck am I supposed to know? I don't even know what the hell they look like."

"Well, you gotta do something for me right away.

157

We can take care of Hogg later."

"Whatdya mean?"

"You've got to take Jewel over to Woo Fong's house. You're gonna be late as it is. I can't go. You know he won't let me near his place."

"Well, I sure as shit ain't goin'. I got Hogg's blood all over me."

Jubal knew it would do no good to argue with Carl. He was tough as nails. That's why he'd hired him as a strong arm. Jubal would still end up taking Jewel over there. This time, Woo Fong would have to lump it.

The knot on the back of Jubal's head tightened as he stopped his horse in front of Woo Fong's house. He and Jewel had ridden double. There'd been no time to get the carriage out. Pain shot up the back of his head, drove into his brain.

All the way over there, he had planned to dump Jewel off in front of the house and ride away before Woo Fong noticed him, but once he got there, he knew he had to go inside. He had to tell Fong about Hogg and the aborted mission, the mutilated wagon. He dreaded it because he knew Fong would be furious.

Fong would blame him for the foul up. He always did when things went wrong.

As Jubal walked up to the door, he knew that this could mean the end of his relationship with the fat Chinaman. He really didn't care anymore. He still had Valerie. With her, he could make enough money to last him the rest of his life.

A Chinese houseboy opened the door, escorted the couple into Woo Fong's study.

Fong's face flushed with anger when he saw Jubal.

He got up from his chair, stormed over and stood in front of Jubal, his clenched fists raised in the air.

"What in the hell are you doing in my house. I told you to never come here."

"I had to come. To bring Jewel. To talk to you."

"We don't talk here. This is my home. Where's Hogg. He was supposed to bring her over here a half an hour ago."

"That's what I want to talk to you about. Hogg's dead."

"What do you mean, dead?"

Jubal told him everything that Carl had told him. He saved the part about the missing girls until last because he knew that the Chinaman didn't have much respect for another person's life but the girls meant big money to him. Not only that, he knew that Woo Fong had already paid for this batch of girls. That's why he hadn't gone to ship to meet them.

"How could you do this to me, you stupid bastard," Fong bellowed, his big stomach quaking when he spoke.

"I didn't do anything. It just happened."

"It's your fault for sending Hogg alone. Sometimes I wonder why I ever went into business with you."

"Because you need me," Jubal said, surprised by his own boldness.

"You can't do anything right. This is disastrous. Think of all that money we're losing because of your carelessness."

"It isn't so bad. We've got another group of prostitutes coming in on a stagecoach in the morning."

"You'll probably mess that up too."

"No. I'll handle it myself."

"Someone knows about us. Otherwise they wouldn't have killed Hogg and taken the girls from us. Can you think who it might be?"

"No. I don't know how anyone would know about the operation. We're very careful to keep everything secret. Besides the two of us, there are only about five people who know it and we both know we can trust them."

"Maybe one of the whores is leaking information to a customer."

"None of the whores knows what's going on."

"Jewel does. Now that she's heard us talk."

"That's different and you know it. She didn't know a thing until right now."

"Just to be safe, I'm going to change the plans for the whores coming in from Texas. I'm going to arrange for them to switch to the regular stagecoach in the next town. They'll come into San Francisco just like regular passengers. If anyone is watching for them to come in, they'd be looking for a lone stage coming in the back way. Nobody would think to look in the most obvious place. The regular Butterfield stage."

"Good idea," Jubal said, relieved that Fong had let up on him.

"You be sure and meet the stage personally. Your face isn't very well known and it would never do if someone saw me picking up six beautiful women. If anyone recognizes you, they'll just figure you're getting a delivery of new whores. Might be good for business."

Jubal was beginning to relax. The knot on his head

160

was going away.

"You'll be pleased to know that we took in five hundred dollars in tips last night," he said, patronizing the Chinaman. "That added to the three thousand we got just for having the girls there made it a profitable evening. Did you enjoy the party?"

"Yes. Which reminds me, you've got a twin."

"Oh?"

"Yes. One of the servants looked just exactly like you. I had to look twice before I realized it wasn't you. I knew you wouldn't be caught dead wearing one of those silly uniforms."

Jubal felt the flush rise to his face. He knew it was time to leave before Woo Fong had second thoughts.

"I must get back now."

"Yes. Just see that you don't come here again. I will have one of my servants bring Jewel back in the morning."

Jubal heard the commotion as soon as he walked in the doors of the House of Paradise. He hated to show his face, but it sounded like Carl needed help. Now that Hogg was gone, he'd have to fill in until he could get a replacement. He walked from the back door up to the front lobby.

"But she isn't here, I told you," Carl yelled.

"What's the problem here?" Jubal said as he walked in. He was glad to see that Carl had changed clothes.

"This gentleman is demanding to take his pleasures with Jewel. I told him she wasn't here and he's calling me a liar."

"Cool your tempers, fellows. We don't want any

fights in here." He turned to the irate customer. "Carl's right. Miss Jewel is busy tonight. We can give you another girl just as good."

"But she's here isn't she?" said Tom Penrod. "I just want to be with her for a little while. I can hurry if she's busy. It doesn't take me long once I've set my mind to it."

"No, she isn't here. She had another engagement and I just delivered her myself."

"Oh, I didn't know you could take a girl home with you," Tom said, knowing full well that they never let any of the girls out of their sight. "Maybe that's what I should do. Take a girl to my place."

Jubal thought fast.

"No, you don't understand. This customer is crippled. He can't make it to the bordello. As a special courtesy we take the girl to his home. But we don't make a practice of this. We'll be happy to fix you up with one of the other girls."

"No. I want Jewel. I already paid a hundred dollars for her services."

"We can refund your money if you'd like. Or you can take your choice of the others."

"How about both? My hundred back and still get a girl?"

"Since there's been a misunderstanding, I'm going to do just that. Refund your money and you take your choice of the girls. Spend as much time as you want with her." Jubal didn't want any trouble. Not when everything else was going wrong.

"That's good enough for me." Tom figured he might as well take advantage of it. This would probably be the only chance he'd get to visit such an expensive whorehouse.

Tom was taken into another room where the scantily dressed girls were waiting. He looked them over, picked out the rare beauty with hazel eyes, long light brown hair. She took him upstairs to a corner bedroom. A dim rosy glow filled the room.

"What's your name, stranger?" the girl husked as she slinked over to Tom.

"Tom."

"Hi, Tom. I'm Penny." Her voice dripped with honey. She wriggled her hips, slid the straps of her brief bodice down over her shoulders.

"You're very pretty, Penny." Tom unbuttoned his shirt, reached for the breast that jutted out from her blouse. "Penny? Did you say Penny?"

"That's my name." She tiptoed her fingers down Tom's trousers, squeezed the hardening bulge.

"I think I know you. That is, I think my friend knows you."

"I don't want to talk about your friend. I want to talk about you."

"I mean, I think you're the one Bolt was trying to help."

"Bolt. Yes. He's the one."

"He tried to find you. Said he went to get you something to eat and when he got back, you were gone. Damn, he'll be happy to know about this. That you're alive and safe."

"If you call this living. That brute Carl caught up with me after Bolt left and Carl forced me to come back here. It's a living hell. God, I hope he can get us all out of here. I've got so much to tell him. One of the strong arms was killed tonight and it's been a

163

mass confusion here all night. There was a lot of yelling and screaming and I was able to sneak out of my room. I found out about a lot of things tonight.''

"Damn, I wish I could sneak you out of here. Bolt needs all the information he can get. He's planning on getting all of you girls out of here and maybe you're the one who can help him.''

"We might be able to get away with it tonight. With Hogg dead, there's only two of them to watch us. And I know one of them has to take care of the body. So that leaves only one. Someone always stays with the girls when we are in that room downstairs.''

"Penny, you got any other clothes? A long skirt?''

"Yes.'' She showed him the clothes in her closet.

"Perfect.'' He drew out her dark shawl, a long skirt and a blouse.

"What good is that going to do?''

"Penny, can you look like a man?''

"After working here, I can look like anything.''

Tom stripped out of his clothes, handed them to Penny. "Here, put these on.''

When they had finished dressing in each other's clothes, Tom checked her, told her to wear his jacket. He placed his hat on her head, tucked her hair up under it.

Penny walked over to the window, looking down below.

"Carl's horse is gone, so they've taken the body away.''

"Then we're set.''

"But your hair. You don't look like a woman with that short hair.''

"That's the idea.''

Penny shrugged her shoulders.

"Now, you go down first. Just act natural like you were me leaving. You'll have to go by that room where the girls are and I'm figuring that Jubal will be in there with them. The door's open so keep your head kind of turned away as you go by. Go on out the front door, turn right and go to the first corner. Go around the corner, out of sight, and wait for me. I'll be there in about five minutes."

Penny walked down the stairs, took a deep breath, headed for the front door. She saw Jubal's form appear in the doorway on her left just before she got there. Her heart pounded in her chest, but she kept right on walking. She turned her head to the side, brushed imaginary lint from her trousers as she passed the door. She knew Jubal was watching her.

"Good night," Jubal called.

She didn't dare answer him. Instead, she raised her left arm and waved. It was an effort not to run to the front door, but she forced herself to walk until she was out of the front door. When she turned the corner, she almost collapsed from fear. The next five minutes would be the longest five minutes in her life.

Chapter Sixteen

Tom waited the five minutes and then he was ready to go. He wasn't at all worried about his part in this charade.

He clunked down the stairs, his feet pinched inside Penny's shoes. Jubal appeared in the doorway, as Tom knew he would.

Jubal stared down the hallway at Tom, thought it was one of his girls for an instant. He started to move out of the room, did a double-take, looked closely at Tom's face and hair, realized that he was looking at the man who had caused such a commotion before.

"What the hell's going on here?" he snapped.

Tom stopped when he got to the doorway, stood a few feet away from Jubal.

"That's one hell of a gal you've got up there," he said. He reached down grabbed the skirt and pulled it out to the side as if to show it off. "She'll do any damn thing you ask her to. Never had so much fun in

166

my life. You train your girls good here."

Tom let the skirt fall back to his side. He saw Jubal shudder, then step out into the hall to watch him in disbelief. Before Tom reached the front door, it opened and two distinguished looking men entered.

"Good evening, fellows," Tom said. "You'll have a ball here tonight." It was all Tom could do to keep from laughing when he saw the shocked expressions on their faces. When he stepped outside, Tom knew he had pulled it off.

Jubal would be busy for quite a while. Explaining to the two gentlemen what kind of a house he ran.

Bolt had a lot to tell Merle Stamps the next morning when he met him for breakfast as they had planned. He had stayed up late talking to Penny and Tom, laughing about the stunt they pulled to get Penny out of the whorehouse. When it was time to go to bed, Penny had gone with Tom. And Tom deserved her. He had really come through for Bolt this time and only Tom was clown enough to carry it off.

"You've been right on every count so far," he told Stamps. "Woo Fong's the top man. Penny didn't know anything about a stagecoach coming in this morning, but other than that she knows all about their operation. We still have to get the rest of the girls out of there and kick Fong and Jubal out of town or shut them down, but with all the facts we've got, it shouldn't be hard. They ought to be locked up for the rest of their lives."

"That won't be easy. The sheriff and the mayor are just like this." Stamps crossed his fingers, held them up in the air. "Unless we can get the sheriff to lean our way, those two crooks won't even be arrested."

"Maybe we should pay him a call this morning, remind him of the papers you got on him."

"We don't need him. We stop Woo Fong from doing business, and Kalloch loses his power anyway. I swear my boss is going to kill the mayor one of these days. I got papers on you, too, Bolt."

"Oh?"

"Wanted posters."

Bolt tilted his head, shrugged his shoulders.

"I'm impressed. Haven't run into one of those for three years. I'll tell you all about it one of these days."

"I'm sure I'll be the one to be impressed."

"What about the stagecoach? You think Woo Fong will have the girls brought in by some back road?"

"I reckon they'll arrive on the regular stage. There's one due in at eight thirty this morning."

"That means someone will be meeting them then."

"That means we ride out and meet the stage before it gets here. We can take my horse and buggy to tote 'em back."

"The stage comes up from Los Angeles doesn't it? Yes, it does because Tom and I followed that route when we came up here. Why not take a driver with us, let him take them back to Los Angeles where they can catch another stage back home?"

"Good idea," Stamps said.

"Those girls will disappear before they get here."

At eight-thirty that morning, Bolt and Tom sat in a restaurant across the street from the stage stop. They had a window table and a perfect view of the other side of the street.

"There he is now," Stamps said.

"It's Jubal. You owe me a dollar."

"I thought for sure it would be the Chinaman." Stamps fished out a dollar bill, slid it across the table to Bolt.

"Would be a snap to pick him off now." Bolt made his hand into the shape of a pistol, pointed the index finger at Jubal, sighted him in with his thumbnail.

"Too damned easy. I like a challenge."

The stagecoach was ten minutes late. They knew it would be. Since the girls did not have any luggage, it had taken Bolt and Stamps only ten minutes to transfer the girls to the other coach, bribe the driver to tell anyone who asked that he didn't know anything about six beautiful women.

They watched Jubal pace up and down the boardwalk in front of the small stagecoach building, stop and rub the back of his head at times. At least once a minute, sometimes twice, he fished the gold watch out of his watchpocket, check the time, jam the watch back in its slit and look to the south.

As the coach approached, they saw him wring his hands, lick his lips and look all around him to see if anyone was waiting to snatch the girls away from him as they had done the night before.

The driver came in at an angle which was perfect for Bolt and Stamps. They could see one side of the coach, most of the other side. Jubal waited for the driver to climb down and open the doors. Bolt could see that the curtains were drawn across the window on their side of the coach, knew the other window was covered too.

Instead of going back to the stage door, the driver went up to the front of the coach, got down on his hands and knees and tinkered with the heavy wooden wheels. Jubal waited for a minute or so, rubbed the back of his neck, stretched his neck to look at the window. In pantomime, they saw Jubal approach the driver, speak to him, point to the stagecoach door. The driver got up off his knees, dug into one pocket, then another one, patted the back pockets, the front of his shirt, then shrugged his shoulders, palms of his hands turned upward. Jubal was mad when he spoke to the driver. It showed in his face.

The driver suddenly remembered something. He was smiling now, pointing to his jacket that was still in the seat, telling Jubal that he had left the keys to the stage in his jacket.

By this time Bolt and Stamps were in stitches, their jaws aching from laughing so hard.

While the driver checked his jacket pockets, Jubal walked over to a window, pressed his ear against it. A frown crossed his face and he tried it again. When he got back to the front of the stage, the driver was shaking his head, showing Jubal the empty pockets. Jubal was screaming now, shaking his fist. As the driver climbed down again, Jubal looked down at the ground, walked around the front, to near side, stretched his neck to check the seat, then went back to the other side and screamed ome more.

A wide grin spread across the driver's face. He
pointed to the ground near the wheel he had been
working with. He stooped down, picked up a set of
keys and held them high in the air. Before Jubal
moved toward the door, he looked all around him,
checked everywhere but the restaurant across the
street.

And then the moment they had all been waiting for
when the driver unlocked the door, threw it wide
open. Jubal smiled, watched the door with anticipation. A minute later, a look of horror came over his
face. He stepped closer to the coach door, stuck his
head inside, looked right, left, up, down.

Then there were the words, the shouts, the
threatening fist. The only thing the driver did for the
next two minutes was shake his head and shrug his
shoulders. Jubal finally lowered his face to his hands,
shook his head, then mounted his horse and rode
away.

"Tom couldn't have done it better," Bolt said. He
dashed across the street, Stamps on his heels.

"You ought to be an actor," Bolt said.

"I am," said the driver. "Name's Mike Murphy.
I'm a pantomime artist at the Beach Front Theatre.
Well, I knew who you were talking about when you
told me to tell anyone who asked that I didn't know
anything about those six girls. I carried Jubal's girls
once before, but they had a guard and there was
nothing I could do about it. But I heard the girls
talking. Fact is, just before you reached me this
morning I had decided to turn back. I just couldn't
be a part of it."

"Well, you gave it your all. I've never seen anything so funny."

"Why do you think I drove the coach in at that angle? I knew you'd be in there watching Jubal's reaction to the empty stage. That show was for you. My appreciation for sending those girls back home."

"Now what?" the young Stamps asked when he and Bolt were mounting their horses.

"I think we'd better move in on 'em tonight. I have a feeling all hell's gonna break loose after this caper. In fact we might not have to worry about it. Woo Fong will probably be ready to kill Jubal himself after losing two loads of prostitutes."

"Need some help?"

"Be nice if you hung around on the outskirts so you could get the story, but I don't want you getting hurt in the melee. Tom'll be with me and I think any more than that would confuse the issue."

"Let me know when or where and I'll cover it."

"You going to work today?"

"Yeah. I'll be at the paper all day."

"I've been thinking about something I saw yesterday and I might need you to go with me to use a little of your special persuasion tactics."

"Got anything to do with the kidnap ring?"

"In a way. I'll let you know if I go."

Bolt rode back to the hotel alone. He needed some time to think. The situation at the Snyder ranch had been heavy on his mind. He wasn't sure if it was any of his business, but he couldn't get Chin's sad face out of his mind. When he thought about the thing Snyder did to Chin's sister, he wanted to vomit. H

172

wondered if Snyder had ever violated his own daughter, Annabelle. She was certainly sexually oriented. But he wasn't worried about her. She was strong and independent, able to take care of herself.

He knew no one else would do anything about the situation. Not the sheriff or mayor, certainly. Not any of Snyder's peers. He didn't even know why he was asking himself these questions. He already knew what he was going to do.

When he got back to the hotel, he told Tom that he wanted to make the strike that night. He didn't want those girls to be locked up another night. He wanted to take Jubal and Woo Fong in custody and keep them under wraps until he could send for a circuit judge who would be impartial and fair.

"How are you going to get the two of them together?" Penny asked. "The Chinaman won't set foot inside the bordello."

"Then we'll just pick up Woo Fong at his place," said Tom.

"It would be better if they were together," Bolt said. "I've got an idea how I can get the Chinaman to go over to the whorehouse, but I may need your help, Penny."

"I'll do anything I can. You saved me, after all."

"I don't want you to do it for me. I want you to do it for all those other girls."

"Sure."

"Be ready to go about seven. I've got something to take care of before I change my mind."

* *

Bolt explained the situation at the Snyder ranch to Merle Stamps on the way out, told him what he wanted him to do.

"The same kind of scare tactics you used on Mayor Kalloch."

"I've known about the Snyder thing for quite a while, but I didn't realize how bad it was. I'll scare the hell out of him."

Bolt hoped Annabelle wouldn't be there, but she greeted them at the door.

"Back for seconds?" she teased when she saw Bolt.

"Not really. I'd like to talk to your father."

Annabelle looked around Bolt, saw Merle Stamps standing there.

"Oh, are you going to do a story on Daddy's horses? That'll please him."

"I don't think he's going to be pleased at what I have to say, but I want to say it."

"Aw, you're gonna give him a lecture about the servants, aren't you? He'll just laugh at you if you tell him that you pay your whores. Maybe not out loud, but he'll think you stupid. You're not going to change his mind. Why not forget it?"

"Because I think it's important. I think your mother should hear it, too."

"What about me?"

"I'd rather you weren't present."

"Hell, I heard it all yesterday from you. I can sit through it again. Everybody treats me like a kid. And you know I'm all grown up."

"Suit yourself."

Annabelle took them into the living room, told them she would go upstairs and get her parents.

"Would you like a drink while I'm gone? I can have Chin bring the tray."

"No. You know I'm going to be talking about the servants. I don't want any of them in here."

Annabelle left them alone, said she would be right back.

"I hope this works," Stamps said.

"It has to. If you saw the look in that poor Chinese girl's eyes, you'd know what I mean."

"How do they get away with it?"

"Money. Status. Annabelle said that all of the rich people buy their servants at the auctions. As long as nobody complains, they do it. I'm hoping that if I can crack Snyder, then I can find out what other families have bought servants. I'd like to see them all free."

Bolt stopped talking when he heard the footsteps on the stairs. When Annabelle came into the room, Bolt noticed that she had changed her blouse, now wore one that clung to her figure. Her breasts spilled over the top of the blouse where she had left the first three buttons undone.

The Snyders sat on the long couch across from the chairs where Bolt and Stamps were sitting. Bolt had chosen his chair just for that reason.

"Annabelle said you want to lecture us," Joseph Snyder said. "What have you got on your mind?"

"Are you aware that slavery is against the law, Mister Snyder?"

"Of course I am."

"And are you aware that you're breaking the law?"

"You mean because I have hired help, ten of them to be exact, who help me around my ranch and take care of the house.''

"No, I'm not talking about that.''

"See, I told you, Daddy,'' Annabelle sighed.

"Hush, Annabelle. I want to hear what Bolt has to say.''

Bolt noticed that Catherine Snyder, Annabelle's mother, sat quietly between them, her hands in her lap.

"You don't have hired help around here, Mister Snyder.''

"I paid for them.''

"You bought them. That's illegal.''

"What you're saying is that they are slaves because I give the orders and they do what I say. Well that's the way it works in all households. The boss gives the orders. The servants, or hired help follow the orders.''

"You're clouding the issue.''

"Bullshit. It's clear to me.''

"You call them hired help. I call them slaves. Do you pay them a salary or a wage?''

"No, I already told you, I paid for them.''

"If you don't pay them, they are slaves. It's that simple.''

"Mister Snyder,'' Stamps interrupted, "I'm doing a story for our paper. May I quote you?''

"Hell, no, you can't quote me.''

"If you won't admit that you own slaves,'' Bolt said, "let's talk about something else. And I'm not even going to mention the times you beat your servants.''

Snyder shifted positions.

"Have you ever slept with one of your servants''

176

the Chin girl, forced her to have intercourse with you?"

Catherine gasped.

"No," he snapped.

"I have witnesses who say different."

"It's their word against mine."

"Have you ever slept with your own daughter?" Bolt was playing on a hunch now.

Catherine looked at her husband with hate in her eyes.

"No! No, I haven't slept with Annabelle."

"Yes you have, Daddy. Why aren't you honest about it? I am. Besides, they wouldn't dare print that in their paper."

Catherine broke into tears, her body trembling with the sobs.

"Okay. Yes, yes, I'm guilty of everything you say I am, but please don't put it in the paper. I'll sue if you do."

"You can't if it's true," Stamps said.

"We have no intention of putting it in the paper if you cooperate with us."

"That's blackmail."

"It may be but you have a choice."

"What do you want me to do?"

"What you should have done all along. Let your servants go. Pay them a fair wage for every hour they've ever worked for you."

"It would cost me a fortune."

"Make up your mind. We are leaving right away."

"Is that all?"

"That and give me a list of anyone you know who has bought servants at the auction."

"Yes, I'll do it."

"You'll feel much better when you do. And I guarantee no one will ever know about this except the five of us. Thank you. You're a bigger man than I thought."

Chapter Seventeen

Bolt rode up to Valerie's house alone. He wanted to make sure she was all right. He didn't know what would happen that night and he wanted to see her once more before then.

"Hi," she said when the maid brought him into the kitchen, "I was just thinking about you."

"Good thoughts, I hope."

"My father had just mentioned he was going into town to talk to you. He's upstairs getting ready now. He'll be down in a minute."

"Good. Just one quick question before he gets here. Do you like Merle Stamps, the reporter?"

"Are you kidding? I've had a crush on him since I was fourteen years old. We went to school together and he was the first boy who ever kissed me. He's so much more fun to be with than any of my friends, but I don't get to see him that often. He'll always be my first love even though we've gone our different directions. You're darned right I like

Merle Stamps?"

"I didn't ask for your whole life history," Bolt laughed. "Just a simple yes or no."

Rodney Blair entered the room, buttoning his shirt.

"Just the man I wanted to see," Rodney said. "What's this about Merle Stamps?"

"Nothing you'd understand, Father. I'll leave you two alone so you can talk."

Rodney poured two cups of coffee without asking, set one of them in front of Bolt. He sat down across the table from Bolt, took a sip of coffee before he spoke.

"I've got serious troubles, Bolt. Nothing you can help me with, but I wanted to talk it out and you're the only one I trust."

"Go ahead and talk. I'm a good listener."

"For some time now I've had an inkling that the bank books weren't balancing. I'm pretty good with figures and I usually know what the accounts should look like without having to go through a lot of paperwork. I did some checking and found out that several of the accounts were short. I dug in a little deeper and found out that I was missing more than I thought I was. So I paid to have an audit done on the books last week."

"How much were you short?"

"Over thirty thousand dollars when the audit was done."

"That's a lot of money."

"The audit was finished on Thursday. And on Friday, another three thousand was pilfered out of the funds."

"Got any idea who did it?"

"Yes. The auditors found two sets of books. I recognized the handwriting. It was Emory Howes, my very best friend."

"You know, in a way, I'm not really surprised."

"But I've helped him out so often. Why would he do this to me? I've loaned money when he's needed it. I brought him out and gave him a decent job. I just don't understand it."

"There are some people you can't help. Even best friends. The more you help them, the more dependent they become on you. Gradually, they begin to expect it of you and when you don't deliver, they take what they think is theirs. I'm not saying this is what Emory did, but he's a very insecure man."

"If he needed money, why didn't he just ask for it?"

"I don't know, but sometimes you do a person a favor by not helping them out when they ask. Makes them stand on their own two feet. Makes them stronger because they did it themselves."

"But I only helped Emory out when he was desperate. I couldn't let him starve to death."

"Maybe I'm far enough away from the relationship between you and Emory to see what happened. You brought him out here, gave him a job, probably loaned him money to get set up here."

"Right."

"Every time you gave him something, you took away a little of his manhood. In other words, he felt less of a man when you helped him out because he hadn't done it himself. Not your fault. You were doing it out of genuine concern for a friend. But the more you gave him, the less he felt like his own man."

"I understand what you're saying."

"Sometimes it backfires on you, too. You give a man some money the first time, he is grateful. The second time he feels that you are better than he is because he could not reciprocate and help you too. On and on until finally, he resents you because you are such a big man and he is so little, even though he has done this to himself."

"Then they try to bring you down a little so they will be bigger."

"You understand it. You just had to hear someone else say it."

"But why would he embezzle three thousand dollars on Friday? He certainly couldn't have needed it. He wore his old suit to the party. You'd think if he had that kind of money, he'd have had a new suit made."

"Three thousand, you say? I know exactly what he used it for."

"What?"

"You're not going to like it."

"What?"

"Did you know that a bordello was set up out back the night of the party?"

"In the cottages? No, I don't believe it. I would have known it if there had been."

"No you wouldn't. Emory said not to mention it to you because you were stuffy about such things."

"What did Emory have to do with it?"

"More than I thought at the time. He took Tom and me out there, told us to help ourselves, that the services were free to all the guests."

"I find this very hard to believe."

"Not as hard as you're going to. It will probably shock you to know that your bank paid for the services of all of the prostitutes."

"What?"

"The cost of furnishing the prostitutes was three thousand dollars. I knew that one of the wealthy men at the party had paid for them, but I didn't know at the time that it was Emory. By the way, does Emory have any servants?"

"Yes, about six of them."

"Can he afford them?"

"I don't see how. We are quite comfortable paying two servants, but any more would put a strain on us."

"I have a feeling Emory has slaves, not servants. I think he stole money from the bank to buy slaves. He isn't paying them any wages. That's what your friend, Joe Snyder has done. I just talked to him. He's going to pay for every hour they worked for him, but he got away with it for a long time before anyone questioned him about it."

"It's going to take me a long time to sort all this out. I'm so confused and shocked."

"Shocked, maybe, but not confused. You are the only man I know who is completely comfortable with himself. You don't need to steal money or feel guilty because you have slaves or feel guilty because some other man happens to have a little more than you do. You are your own man. You have dignity. No one can ever take it away from you except yourself."

"Thank you for that."

"Now I have one question for you," Bolt said. "Why won't you let Merle Stamps court your daughter? They are both old enough to know what they want."

"I've told Valerie why! He just isn't in the same social circle that we are. Not that he isn't a nice boy, but he just doesn't fit in with our friends or life-style."

"Would you rather she married someone like Emory Howes who finds it necessary to steal from his best friend just to prove he's a man? Would you rather she marry a duplicate of Joe Snyder who besides being a slave owner, sleeps with his maid and even his own daughter?"

Bolt saw Rodney's face blanch white.

"These are the men who are in your social circle, who are on the same level with you, who fit in with your friends. That's the kind of a man you're telling me you want for your daughter."

"I've been a prick, haven't I?"

"Yes, but a damned nice one."

"I wish there was something I could do to help you. You've been so kind to us."

"There is. Not for me, but I think it would be very nice if your circle of friends donated enough money to get Mister Talbott back on his feet."

"You've got it. Bolt, just one more thing. What am I going to do about Emory? He doesn't know that I know."

"What would you do if he was not your friend?"

"I would fire him and and have him arrested."

"That is the only way you can be a friend to him now."

184

"But it would hurt me to do that."

"It might hurt you, but it is the only way you can help him. It will knock him down for a while, but next time he'll get up by himself and he'll be the man he's always wanted to be."

Bolt dropped Penny off a half a block from Woo Fong's home, then rode on to the House of Paradise where Tom was waiting for him. They would not go inside the bordello until they were sure Woo Fong was there. If Penny did her job right, Fong would be there in less than fifteen minutes.

An hour before, Merle Stamps had positioned himself outside the whorehouse, two doors down so he could not be seen from the inside. He carried a large notepad and a pencil, had a card that said "Press" stuck inside the brim of his hat. Each time a potential customer approached the bordello Stamps asked the same question. He said: "Pardon me, sir, we are doing an article on what it feels like to sleep with a whore. Would you care to comment?"

It had worked. Not a single customer had entered since he'd been there. That's what Bolt wanted, all of the girls together in the downstairs room.

Penny ruffled her hair before she went up to Woo Fong's door. The Chinese houseboy let her in as he had done at other times when he had been the chosen one.

"Oh, Woo Fong, you've got to help me," she cried when she ran into his study, unannounced. She took deep breaths, made it look like she was short of wind.

"What's the matter, Penny? How did you get over here?"

"It's Jubal. He's gone crazy. He's holding an auction over at the bordello. He's selling off all the girls and I don't want him to sell me to that brute who wants to buy me."

"Why would he do a thing like that?"

"He said something about feeling bad about losing those last two groups of prostitutes. He said you were mad so he wants to sell all of us and take the profits for himself. Please you've got to come now before any of the girls are sold. He hasn't even let any customers in today. Hurry!"

Bolt saw Woo Fong and Penny dash up to the back door of the bordello and knock on the door.

"Who's there?" called Jubal through the locked door.

"It's Penny," she answered before Woo Fong could respond.

"What in the hell are you doing out there?" he said when he opened the door.

Woo Fong pushed his way inside, shoved Jubal hard, kept shoving him until both men were in Jubal's office.

Bolt and Tom slipped in the back door, stood in the hall by Jubal's office.

"You're not going to sell any of these girls," Woo Fong shouted. "They belong to me, you bastard."

"What are you talking about, you crazy fool?"

"You didn't lose that load of girls last night. The

ones that came in by stage this morning, either. You thought you could keep 'em for yourself and sell them. I'll kill you for this."

"I'm not selling any girls out from under you," Jubal protested.

"Oh, yes you are," said Bolt as he stepped inside the room, his pistol aimed between them.

Both men drew their pistols, but did not shoot at him. Penny ran down the hall when Bolt entered the room. She told Carl to come quick, that Woo Fong was killing Jubal.

He left the girls alone, ran to help his boss.

Penny herded the girls out the front door where Merle Stamps was waiting with a wagon to whisk them away.

"You were trying to kidnap Valerie Blair the night of the party, Jubal. Deny that. You had grand plans of renting her out for big money and then ransoming her back to her parents."

Jubal's gun wavered. He aimed it at Bolt.

"Go ahead and shoot me. It won't do any good. Woo Fong knows I'm telling the truth. He saw you there dressed up in that uniform."

"That was you, you dirty bastard." Woo Fong shot point blank at Jubal.

As Jubal started to fall to the floor, he turned his gun, shot Woo Fong in the head.

Bolt turned away from the dead men, suddenly exhausted.

"You can have it all," he said to Carl who stood in the doorway, shocked. "There's nothing left anymore. No girls, no money. But you can have it all."

Bolt and Tom went back to the hotel, but they didn't spend the night.

Bolt didn't know where he was when dawn broke the next morning. He didn't care.

Freedom was his home. It always had been.

THE SURVIVALIST SERIES
by Jerry Ahern

#1: TOTAL WAR (960, $2.50)
The first in the shocking series that follows the unrelenting search for ex-CIA covert operations officer John Thomas Rourke to locate his missing famly—after the button is pressed, the missiles launched and the multimegaton bombs unleashed . . .

#2: THE NIGHTMARE BEGINS (810, $2.50)
After WW III, the United States is just a memory. But ex-CIA covert operations officer Rourke hasn't forgotten his family. While hiding from the Soviet occupation forces, he adheres to his search!

#3: THE QUEST (851, $2.50)
Not even a deadly game of intrigue within the Soviet High Command, the formation of the American "resistance" and a highly placed traitor in the new U.S. government can deter Rourke from continuing his desperate search for his family.

#4: THE DOOMSAYER (893, $2.50)
The most massive earthquake in history is only hours away, and Communist-Cuban troops, Soviet-Cuban rivalry, and a traitor in the inner circle of U.S. II block Rourke's path. But he must go on—he is THE SURVIVALIST.

#5: THE WEB (1145, $2.50)
Blizzards rage around Rourke as he picks up the trail of his family and is forced to take shelter in a strangely quiet Tennessee valley town. Things seem too normal here, as if no one has heard of the War; but the quiet isn't going to last for long!

Available wherever paperbacks are sold, or order direct from the Publisher. Send cover price plus 50¢ per copy for mailing and handling to Zebra Books, 475 Park Avenue South, New York, N.Y. 10016. DO NOT SEND CASH.